THE MAN WHO KNEW TOO MUCH

A STORY ABOUT A QUEST FOR KNOWLEDGE

BY RICHARD STEWART

*To all my friends and family
who have had an impact on my life.*

INTRODUCTION

Alfred is a man on a mission, what mission I'm not sure and I'm not sure if he knows either.

But this is a story about Alfred on his journey for a quest for knowledge and how he dramatically shares it with others around him.

Now, here's a little story
to tell it is a must
about a man named Alfred
that helps move away the dust
some people are a headache
others are quite thick
but Alfred flips a hose a lot
in fact, he's flippin' quick.

Yes, Alfred is the man of the hour. It depends which hour you catch him in.

Born and bred in Queensland somewhere, we don't know where, he hasn't told us yet. But in time, he will make a living through mining operations. A fitter by trade, a hose spinner by night and a vehicle builder by day.

The essential tools for Alfred are a hammer and a shifter. He can explain the use of these combinations in great detail to anyone who will sit down and listen.

Yes, Alfred's experience as a fitter you will see is phenomenal. How he prepares the simplest of tasks in detail, as you will find out from cover to cover, into the most intriguing builds you will ever see.

Group or pass meetings before the work shift starts, Alfred always has a safety share.

"Stay focused on the job. If you're unsure, I may be able to help."

The supervisor will always round off the conversation with the day's or night's events and thank Alfred for contributions.

To everyone in the team, he is the patriarch, not sure if they know what means, but he is always acknowledged with a thumbs up.

For anyone who feels discouraged, Alfred has these simple words to offer. "Dah dah dah dah dah dah dah. Don't worry, be happy. Don't worry, be happy."

Just simple words to sing along to are enough to make a grown man cry.

This is Alfred, a very caring man, very expressive in his thinking, and if there is something he doesn't agree with, he will certainly tell you. You'll find out later when it comes to horse racing.

But there will be times when no one knows where Alfred is, especially on a night shift. When he eventually comes back to the workshop and is questioned, his favourite answer is, you guessed it: "I've been counting sheep."

And when questioned again: "With eyes open or shut?"

The answer would always come back the same: "A combination of both."

The reality check was the question, "Where were the sheep, Alfred?"

"The farmer came and removed them just before I was going to close the pen."

Unfortunately, sheep don't hang around coal mines. So losing your sanity for a few hours in relieving some stress is a good thing, Alfred always thought.

This is Alfred's story, a peak performer, always reliable. We don't know exactly where he lives but he's always reliable.

Men like Alfred are hard to find in this day and age. But if you happen to find a man like Alfred, he is worth his weight in gold.

Hang on a minute, Alfred doesn't have any gold. It's a nice

thought, though.

One last thing I'll mention as an introduction to Alfred's journey: he smiles a lot. That's when you catch him in the mood.

Alfred's a man's man. A solid rock you can bounce off, a pillar not a pillow.

ALFRED'S STORY

In the beginning

Alfred was born in the late 1900s and this was now 2022. You could say he has lived in two centuries which he has, like many of us. The tale of two centuries. A veteran Queenslander by birth. We found out that he had grown up in a place called Winton, Central Queensland. Winton, where there is no winter. A farming community, but Alfred was no farmer. He had grown up thinking he could become a specialist. As specialist in what though?

In his early years, he was nurtured by his parents and siblings to think outside the square. And he quite often thought, *What is the square?*

What! Farming is not thinking outside the square.

You need to have the qualities of a free man, a man who could fix anything with a shifter and a hammer. It had never occurred to Alfred that there was great potential in making a wise decision like this.

In Alfred's formative years, he began to develop skills in dismantling mechanical machinery and when it came time to put the pieces back together again, he always had a few pieces left over. It had occurred to him he had modified the equipment without the manufacturing instructions. The asset would work great till there was no oil left in the engine sump. He had not placed the engine oil sump in the right place or maybe that was the spare part left over.

These were the early years for Alfred. He not only excelled in the mechanical areas but was a keen sportsman, especially when it came to horse racing, which we will elaborate later in the story so not to cause confusion.

Alfred enjoyed his growing up years in the farming country of

Winton. He loved riding horses, especially wild horses. Alfred told me once he roped this wild horse, trying to break it in with a saddle. Every time he got near the brumby, the brumby would flick the saddle off. So in frustration he got on the brumby bare back. The brumby got such a fright with Alfred's weight, all of 95 kg, it took off with Alfred. Alfred was not seen for several days. Finally when he did get home, Alfred made the comment, "Well, I guess I'm not the horse whisperer."

Alfred came to the conclusion horses had a mind of their own. And as they say, don't get drunk riding a horse, as the fines are a bit steeper than the average drunk driver. Why?

Because in the eyes of the law, a horse has a mind of its own and it could be a real problem on the road.

Alfred took this law very seriously. So you can see now Alfred was a serious non-drinking horseman. It was a different story when the horse got drunk.

These formative years stood him in good stead for the experiences he could pass on to his working colleagues, as we shall see later in the story.

In his later schooling or high school years a career counselor worked with Alfred to place him in a trade. And every day, Alfred would bring his prized hammer and shifter to school. The career advisor commended him for his enthusiasm in the engineering field and gave him a heads up not to bring a hammer and a sickle or wear a red scarf. When Alfred asked why, the career advisor would say, "Never you mind, the authorities will deal with that."

Alfred began to break records in the school engineering workshop for his projects and he also began breaking lathes. Alfred was trying to manufacture a square bit of steel to suit a round hole. He still could not get his thinking outside the square, till the engineering teacher had a word with him and drew a picture of a round object in a round hole. This made perfect sense. Alfred went on to top his class in the engineering workshop program that year, and his name will be forever remembered on the outstanding achievers' board sitting outside the wood workshop.

You might ask why outside the wood workshop and not the engineering workshop. Alfred's name would not be inscribed on the plaque till two years later. It was a wood plaque.

Alfred was given a highly recommended critique for his work. A highly recommended future candidate to become part of your company.

Alfred's last project in the workshop alongside his colleague on the bench next to him was to build a boat. The task had been assigned to both students. His friend Angus was building a model boat. Now thinking outside the square, Alfred was building a huge ship. Alfred was taking this thinking outside the square to its extremes. Receiving an A for his project, Alfred left school that year with honours and his ship.

Alfred's parents and siblings were proud of Alfred and his accomplishments at school. One small problem: they didn't know where to berth the ship Alfred had built. Maybe it could be used as accommodation till the next outback flood, then they could float or power it up to the closest coastal port, Townsville or Mackay, depending on the current.

When Alfred was asked why he had built rather a large boat, he replied, "I got my inspiration from Noah. His dimensions were about the same size as the 'Winton Princess.'"

But Noah carried animals. "Yes, the animals will come later, I'm still waiting for the flood here in Winton."

Alfred didn't have to wait long as in the next few months, a massive amount of water was unleashed from the heavens and the Winton Princess was promptly steered into the Mackay Harbour. You could say as a young achiever Alfred was "floating his stock."

7

THE EARLY DAYS IN
THE REAL WORLD OF WORK

Employers were quickly keen to pick up Alfred for the apprenticeship of his choice. Alfred didn't even have to open his mouth. His reputation even at an early age preceded him. His toolbox represented the hammer and the shifter with of course a few little

other incidentals that made the toolbox seem heavy. He remembered what his career advisor had said a year or two ago about a hammer and a sickle, but why did he have to remove the Russian flag sticker off his toolbox?

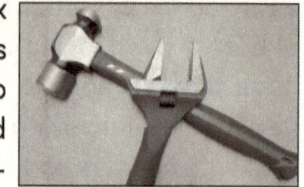

Then there was Horse. He had started his apprenticeship the day after Alfred. Horse was a big strong guy with a high-pitched woman's voice. As Alfred was given his small tasks to do with his tradesmen at his side, there would be Horse. A woman trapped in a man's body. Alfred managed to try and refrain himself, but his Uncle Chuck had given him a reminder and he would use it on Horse if he got too close. "I was once a man trapped in a woman's body. Then I was born."

Alfred couldn't help himself and next time Horse came leaning around, out came the quotation. This didn't go down well. Horse, very upset, asked if he could be relocated to another BMA site.

Alfred was becoming a man's man. How do we know that? We don't know, only he does.

The amount of vehicle pieces lying around the light vehicle workshop on site was incredible. Alfred had not forgotten the skill of making vehicles lighter and having spare parts left over. Vehicles went faster and the oil sump was always checked to ensure it was there. But there was an increase in light vehicle accidents on mining access roads. The pre start records of every vehicle involved in accidents had been filled out correctly, but claimed that drivers had been falling asleep at the wheel due to carbon monoxide poisoning.

Alfred remembered seeing a stack of air filters on the workshop floor. Quickly, Alfred, the top apprentice, advised management air filters had been removed and that was the problem. Alfred had forgotten to put them in, not telling anyone, but being quick to find the problem, Alfred won an award.

Alfred would go on to become apprentice of the year. Another title to add to his accolades.

Alfred was fast building a reputation and respect on all other coal mine sites. Word got around.

"Have you seen Alfred? Do you know where he's working?"

"We want Alfred."

There was also a downside to Alfred. He was always in one of two minds. Go fast or go slow.

It was very hard to pick at the beginning of each day, till the adrenaline kicked in.

Then the brain would kick in. Then the complete Alfred would kick in. That's when the conversations went rampant and you began to know what Alfred knows and what he is thinking.

Alfred was a mature apprentice for his age, he covered a lot of ground or coal dirt in the four years of his apprenticeship.

He was even once involved in a light  vehicle incident with an excavator. The excavator operator dropped his glasses while bending over to grab something. Scrambling to find his glasses, he had double vision. Seeing two light vehicles parked, he missed the dump truck and buried Alfred and his tradesmen's vehicle. Everything was let loose: mine sirens, radio sirens, trying to unbury the light vehicle. When the emergency crew eventually got to the cab of the light vehicle, they found Alfred and his tradesmen with their seats reclined sound asleep. The air conditioning is still functioning. Fortunately, it was only half a ton of coal. Three hundred tonnes accidentally dropped may have been a different story.

For this incident, the excavator operator was suspended from all duties pending all investigations.

For Alfred and his tradesmen, they were given paid leave to have a holiday on the company's expense and recuperate from any anxiety that may have been caused, having been checked by the paramedics on-site. That's how valued Alfred and any person working with him was.

Alfred, in his recuperation period now, and nearly a full tradesmen, decided he needed to make that recuperation period last six months on an overseas tour, all on the company. His anxiety pains led him to all great places on the European continent and British Isles. This trip gave Alfred the determination to come home healed from anxiety and become the full tradesmen he wanted to be.

We would hear that story many times over the next ten years from Alfred. Every time it was a little different.

Journeying on, over the course of the next fifteen years, Alfred would move from site to site with the same company BMA. From every site, he had a different story to tell.

But we journeyed with Alfred on a new coal mining site, where he fit in quite well.

LOOK WHO IS
COMING TO NANDI

There were mixed emotions when people of the Nandi mine knew Alfred was joining the team.

They knew he would keep them on their toes as the liaison officer, the fix-it man now.

The fix it man now. When anything needed to be done, Alfred's expertise would come swinging into action, otherwise you wouldn't notice him, as he moved dragging his feet, head down, but in a fraction of a second would lift his manner to un-cover a plot or a situation. Alfred was there when the fuel bowser overflowed at the fuel farm. And how he stopped the spillage of litres of diesel. Yes, off came Alfred's shirt to absorb the con-tents. If that was not enough, off came everyone else's as well. This was a team effort to save the environment on none other than Alfred's watch.

You could say Alfred was the man who came alive at the drop of a hat. The question would always arise: where does he come from, and where is he going? Nobody knows, not even Alfred himself.

Alfred is just there, the expression on his face tells you noth-ing. It's like the lights are left on and stay on, then the room is occupied and a wealth of catalogued information comes out: the biggest haul trucks worked on and how the servicing needs to be down a specific way, according to Alfred, how many generators need to be filled and serviced in a week. Then the topic changes to horse racing, weather, how it affects him and his mood swings.

Alfred is in his element, the explanation to a problem would come from all angles. If there is a feature to be designed or a communication set back, Alfred would be called in. He's the think tank for mining operations on site.

A great example is the hose link operations. How to fill up generators with a short hose over a great distance? An extension made of quarter inch plastic hose pipe attached to the bowser hose, filling a generator diesel tank. This is at night when workmen are tired but not Alfred; he's at peak performance. Alfred had been telling me he's been thinking tonight, what a relief. Does that mean he doesn't think most other nights?

What pearls of wisdom are we expecting tonight?
Then we are reminded again:
Alfred is a fitter.
He wears a fitter's hat.
He wears those baggy trousers
and he has lived in the outback.
He looks a proper miner
in his great big steel-capped boots.
He's got a job to tie them up.
He calls them jackass boots.

When it comes to taking that well-earned lunch break, Alfred could be heard singing, "I want a mixed grill covered in sauce, with enough greasy chips to feed a horse."

"Horse! Please don't remind me of horse," Alfred would say.

Horse was now far away on another mine site.

FITTER BY DAY,
STREAKER BY NIGHT

In Alfred's downtime after work, the bus would pull into the camp. Alfred would race straight to the laundry. Without thinking about it, in went the clothes.

But Alfred, what about the change of clothes to compensate? No clothes, it was better to race to his room, down the corridor wearing nothing but a smile.

...wearing nothing but a smile.
Yes, they do in fact call him the streak.

Alfred was the Entertainer that night and it wouldn't be the last. A lasting impression to many. I hope they were good impressions.

With the day over and the excitement winding down, Alfred begins to reflect on his day with the involvement of others, the operation hose rebuild, and the generators he has miraculously filled and maintained in record time.

Alfred could go to sleep that night knowing he had used his skill and knowledge to help others to achieve their best. And then bring on the entertainment at the camp as the sun was sinking below the horizon.

Alfred was wearing nothing but a smile as he closed his eyes one more time that night. Tomorrow would be a new day, new achievements to aim for, taking pride in his personal best and remembering to replace all those spare parts on the shop floor.

What a day. Could there be any more like them? Alfred thought.

THE GAMBLING MAN
ON THE RUN

The following day, Alfred came to work having arisen from a sturdy sleep. Overnight he had bet on two teams, the underdogs and the highly favoured.

Alfred, you have put odds in your favour. If you lose you don't snooze cause at the other end of the scale you have won. "Always think on the bright side of life."

But to win big, you must play big.

"I've won thirteen dollars either way," said Alfred.

Alfred was now working on his racing results. A photo of proof was to be sent. Alfred had to be commended as Alfred was not a big gambling man, he knew when to hold it, the stakes were high.

Kenny Rogers at this point spoke into Alfred's ear, telling him that he should know when to hold his cards but also when to walk away.

He has a point, Alfred thought.

Then all of a sudden, out of the blue, Alfred would become the hit man. He stumbles out with the whacking machine, the order book to take orders for truck parts.

When does Alfred rest, or doesn't he?

OLYMPICS, HERE ALFRED COMES

Within days on site, Alfred turned and assembled a trolley into a racing bobsled, taking the lead.

By taking the sides off the working trolley, he was sure he could get a team and sponsorship together for the upcoming Olympics in Tokyo. You realise this is a no brainer.

Alfred began to visualise his homecoming song

They're going to put Alfred in the movies.
They're going to make a bobsled team
leader out of him
the fastest bobsledder in the Olympics
and all he has to do with team is act naturally.
Well, I bet you there going to be some big stars
might be in line for an Oscar, just you wait and see.
Well, I hope you come and see Alfred in the movie
then Alfred will know you will plainly see
the biggest laugh that ever hit the big time.
And all that Alfred had to do was act naturally.

The future belongs to the dreamers like Alfred,
not to the critics.

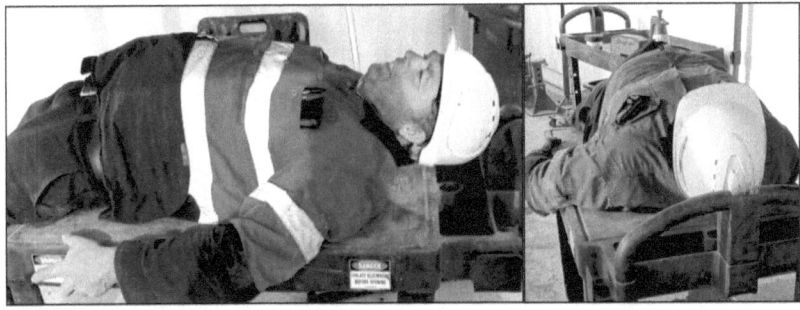

Rich the coach, Alfred the front man, and the team would eventuate. This would be a very brave move as sponsorship from the mine's resources would not come easy. No one else had big dreams and big plans the way Alfred thought. He would be asked questions like:

1) Have you ever done this before?
2) How do you know this will work?
3) A plastic trolley made into a fibre glass body?
4) Six persons required and no one would take up his offer?

Alfred was never razzled or dazzled, he saw what other people didn't see and sometimes it was strange to see what he did see. It got management scratching their heads. For all they themselves knew now, Alfred was becoming a real asset and not a liability to the company. Maybe they could use him as a planner. It had a wide scope and there seemed to be nothing that Alfred could not do.

With his skills on economising machinery parts that weren't required, especially when they had been removed and vehicles had become lighter, he could save the company a lot of money, to point. Then the vehicles would break down and new vehicles and machinery were required.

The forward planning and thinking now of how Alfred could play a very important part in the company structure and rubbing shoulders with senior management, the mining company seemed to be intrigued at this proposition on sponsorship.

No one else could imagine except Alfred. Alfred became the team planner as well and not the cheerleader. He didn't have the qualities, long legs, tight dress, and sporty look. No, Alfred was not a cross dresser and he was very outspoken on that. But we must admit he may have looked good in stockings and high heels. We will leave it there.

Going back, Alfred was a man's man. Alfred called a spade a spade unless you broke the handle, he was straight up, he has the qualities of a leader. Strong, robust, trying to think of some more, it will come to me shortly.

Alfred didn't have to justify anything he did. If he was wrong, he would admit it. If he said he was right, he would also admit he was right too, and that was often. He wasn't intimidated easily.

The bobsled was put on hold for a few weeks, but we will come back to it.

Give Alfred a service truck and he felt right at home. Every generator on site would be filled to the top. Alfred was once again on top of his game and the company knew it. Alfred also knew the way of the future was in professional bobsledding. Finding any bobsledding organisation in the tropics to associate with in central Queensland may be a bit difficult, as it didn't snow or ice up very often in the area.

The too hard basket was never a consideration for young Alfred. Alfred would plough through others' incompetence.

"Give me a hammer and I'll fix it."

It might work in the short term, but in the long term, a requisition order would be noted and part numbers required if the item hadn't been destroyed in the process.

Alfred moved in mysterious circles. He could disappear and suddenly, turning around, he was right in your face, scaring unsuspecting persons. His intention was to ensure safety and at the same time have a sticky beak. Again, any unsuspecting person would be taken aback in shock.

A hazard report would be placed in the next morning pass meeting. "Man collapsed on suspicion of surprise appearance from worker unnamed."

It wasn't something Alfred made a point of doing on a regular basis, but to be fair, Alfred always played by the company rules, no matter what the consequences.

Talking about emergencies, the night the lightning strike hit, Alfred was nowhere to be seen.

A code red had been sent out to all on site and the camp, over the two way.

"This is a code red, all activities to cease and everyone to return to Crib Rooms (lunch rooms) till red alert downgraded."

It was found out later, Alfred had gone under cover. He thought he was under attack by the greenies who were down the road in protest of mining operations in the area.

Fortunately, Alfred didn't take the matter into his own hands or there would have been a few greenies uprooted and replanted permanently.

Alfred had a way of controlling any form of anger in the way of deep breathing and closing his eyes till someone woke him up.

Still on his mind: the bobsled experience. The training program with efforts in the gym on a daily basis. Early morning starts, the running, the long distance power walking and then the hours of training on his newly fibreglass wheeled bobsled as there was on snow with his rag tagged team.

Will give you an update later.

THE PARTY HOUSE

Alfred wanted to have a big homecoming party on his work swing off. Again, sponsorship was a necessity and again by the company under the Nandi brand. Boy, Alfred must have some pull with management.

A big sign outside Alfred's house: "All welcome."

A theme song Alfred wanted played: "Come together right now at Alfred's Place."

The greenies rushed to Alfred's house on the coastal side of Rockhampton, Queensland to find no one.

"Life is good," Alfred would say. "Always think on the bright side of life."

The conversation then centred on the power reticulation for his premises. He needed more power.

Could it be Alfred had underestimated the whole construction thing when he built his castle and a moat around it? His neighbours had lost power at certain times of the day due to Alfred's excessive consumption when at home from work. And now word got around Alfred was going to have a party.

The neighbours were picturing blackouts and had reported their concerns to the local power supply authority. It wasn't that Alfred was a bad neighbour, it was only because his massive creation was excessive and powering a five-storey castle on the beach front came with enormous expense and was a drain on the power reticulation.

Ergon Power knew of this problem and so did Alfred. Alfred was now looking at the costing from a feasibility study of generating his own power either by wind turbine or hydro. Yes, hydro. In doing so, he wanted to set up his own network against all opposition, authorities, and legislation.

Alfred thought if the power companies could extort exorbitant fees, he too could supply his own power to most of the community at half the cost, still make a profit and keep everyone happy. It was a win win.

So with the party dates being set, construction on the windmills and hydropower from the water levels from his lake, having had a portion of the Fitzroy River rediverted to turn his new incoming turbines and the series of wind turbines situated on the highest level of his castle, Alfred estimated he could generate 100MWs of power. This hadn't happened overnight, this had been planned over several months. That's right, months not years.

The only thing keeping the council and environment inspectors from launching into Alfred's castle was the moat around it. The drawbridge was not used for unwelcome visitors.

Let's get back to the story. Alfred also knew about gas wells, and what a conversation. Gas is also important for generating power from gas turbines, although he had little experience running these. And Alfred confessed he knew nothing about them.

"Pull ya head in," said Alfred, "we were locked down due to a red lightning alert." His diplomatic skills were out of this world, being able to negotiate safety concerns without bringing the house down with fits of laughter. And then Alfred had to bring his mother into the conversation.

"Mumma says life is like a box of crumpets, you never know which one you gonna get."

We didn't even know his mamma from a bar of soap and I'm sure she was a nice lady with good intentions. But crumpets! We usually eat them for breakfast.

Alfred had to top it off by saying, "Mumma's always right." Well, maybe she was sometimes. But not on this occasion.

We'll get back to the pool party shortly.

That week passed quickly and with all the frustrations from the neighbours, council and power companies, Alfred sneaked his way back to work.

Back on a day shift with the early start, Alfred was first on the bus, I mean the work bus of course. He had nothing to prove but show he was on top of a new day, expecting great results. In what?

Only Alfred could work that out once again. The thoughts of Alfred were still a mystery.

He even quoted Forrest Gump this time. Instead of using Crumpets he used Chocolates.

Could this be true of Alfred? Did he see things in a different light from the rest of us? There was no other explanation. The highest IQ recorded in recent years is 140. Alfred would have topped this by another ten percent.

The refuelling truck that morning was waiting for Alfred. The parts in the light vehicle workshop were waiting for him to place back together also. Alfred, from the planning point, was set. The time was right, the day was set and there was the peaceful sunrise.

Yes, the sunrise. After the pre start meeting, there was no better place to find Alfred absorbing the freshness of the early morning and the sun peaking over the horizon.

With three chairs and three fellow miners in a secluded area near the operator's crib hut, you find them singing in unison: "Morning has broken, like the first morning." And finishing off with the song, "Love lifts us up where we belong..."

Not sure what Alfred was high on, but he liked to think he was soaring with eagles not congregating with turkeys.

Alfred had a good voice but a rough passage out and he was a little self-conscious of that, but his work mates cheered him on. Not chaired him on.

In the freshness of that morning and the sunrise, it dawned on Alfred he needed some sporting competition for his pool party back at the castle. Racing Ride on Mowers. Alfred could kill two birds with the one stone, racing rideons and mowing the castle grounds at the same time. This could become a regular event and he would never have to mow his lawns again.

"The winner takes it all, the loser takes the fall."

This would create some competitiveness between rivals. It wouldn't matter much to Alfred. He would get his grounds mowed on a regular basis. Alfred would have to come up with was a prize. He thought hard about this as he contemplated his day's activities. Watch this space.

THE CURRENCY CHECK

Now the topic came up about crypto currency and currency as we know it. Alfred had been keen on crypto; the trouble was like every other currency; it was only valued at what anyone was prepared to pay. Paper currency was government legal tender. Crypto was invisible and could not be controlled as it was digital. This was Alfred's explanation. And whilst crypto was riding high, the proceeds of the over inflating value had helped to build King Alfred the Great's five story castle.

Alfred, you have a point, but what about precious metals such as gold and silver, they have value?

Where do we stand with that?

Alfred was always told he was worth his weight in gold, but he didn't have any. Maybe they could change the saying as he was worth his weight in crypto.

Alfred then begins to roll his eyes a little, and then it came out.

"We better buy more crypto currency," said Alfred.

A new coin would be in the process, a new digital currency. Wait for it, it would be called Alfred's coin. Identified only by having Alfred's head on both sides of the coin but like crypto itself, it would be invisible. Backed by Alfred's personal savings and his gambling fetish.

Alfred thought, *I could carry a wallet with invisible currency and all I would have to do is present my identity for any purchases.*

Now the idea of hiding money, not using a bank, came up. Alfred was giving a heads up to avoid banks if possible and buy gold or silver with a map to only those who would be responsible for where the treasure would be hidden. Crypto currency would just be the front running disguise.

This was Alfred's master plan. He had the castle, the treasure, and his unhappy neighbours. *How can I reconcile with them?* Alfred thought. Then the idea came to him.

"I'll invite them to the pool party and ask them at the same time if they would like to become some of my power-generating customers."

At least they would get a good discount, with a free range of power supplied with no additional chargers. Disconnecting from the power company grid would be something of a displeasure to the power supply authority and they would fight the challenge.

Alfred could rest well with that thought, knowing he could go back to work and his neighbours would feel a little happier, not laughing all the way to the bank, but you guessed it, all the way to work. Even with the singing practice, Alfred had concentrated from that early morning sunrise the week previous, Alfred's vocal cords were getting stronger. He would sing:

He'll be coming down the haul road when he comes
He'll be coming down the haul road when he comes
He'll be shooting out those fuel line hoses
to those hungry generators
and the water cannons on those slippery roads.

Alfred had obviously thought this all through.

Logistical manifestation, whatever that means, Alfred thought, *has to work.*

Alfred's mailbox on the other side of the moat had also become extremely full and it wasn't by his fan club either. Before going to work that morning, under disguise of one of the groundsmen, Alfred cleared his letter box only to find several letters from the governing council body insisting his castle were not up to 1300s building specifications and had insisted he make some drastic modifications or else they have no other option but have a demolition company come in to remove Alfred's castle.

Hang on a minute, how could they get across the moat with

the drawbridge up and the high walls of the castle? They were calling his bluff or did they have some other insidious way of getting on to his premises?

The other letters were good news. Alfred and his partner or wife had won two free tickets to the Melbourne Formula One Grand Prix, all expenses paid. Alfred looked at the dates and to his surprise, those dates were the same week as his planned pool party and there was no way he was going to miss his pool party. In good gesture, Alfred would give the tickets to one of his most annoying neighbours down the road to shut him up.

This was Alfred's generosity in full swing.

In that first five years, Alfred had built a circular pond as he would like to call it, twenty meters wide and twenty meters deep. This would help with any flooding that came in the wet season. That had been approved by the council authority. In Alfred's mind, this was his moat. What the council authorities didn't see coming were the stone masons with all their block work riding across the moat with heavy trucks to lay the foundations for King Alfred's castle.

They had company signs all around the inside of the moat: "authentic accommodation being built, cyclone proof." No building inspectors welcome.

Copies of the blueprints had been sent to the council building department. Alfred previously had gone to a library in Bavaria, having travelled through Europe a few years before. Going to the archive department of the library, Alfred got the exact specifications to build a replica of Neuschwanstein castle, brick by brick, block by block. Alfred always thought five or more years ahead. In this case, it was fifteen with the castle blueprints.

Of course the engineers in the building permit office at the council in provincial Queensland were scratching their heads thinking this was a joke and forgot all about Alfred's building plans and applications. A clever move by Alfred, as this gave him not only a few weeks but several years to build his castle and the castle grounds.

Yes, when Alfred builds something, he always builds it big. "Big boats, big castles."

By the time the engineers had finally taken Alfred seriously over the five-year period, it was too late, the castle had been built. *The neighbours, retired people,* thought Alfred, *were building a holiday home with great views. Until the castle had overshadowed some of their views.*

There was no access to the castle, only by personnel invitation. Yes, Alfred had caught the engineers with their pants down. Alfred the Great strikes again.

Yes, Alfred did not lack in confidence or creativity as he thought on his flight that day from the coastal planes of rural Queensland to his treasured mining employment in western Queensland.

There would be no break ins or theft at Alfred's castle as no one except special forces would be smart enough to climb the castle walls. Oh, and at the top were these welcoming spikes.

The mining charter plane had landed at the mining airport that day. Alfred, getting off the plane with his mining colleagues, began making great strides to picking up his luggage from the baggage carousel, which was a tractor and trailer and onwards to the bus. Sitting on the bus, Alfred closed his eyes and reflected on the events of the last few days and the quick getaway from home before being spotted by his neighbours and the council building inspectors. He began once again to plan.

Now with a clear mind, a new day, a new chapter of Alfred's life, the three most important things on Alfred's mind were:

Firstly, had any of the other fitters on the crew previous disturbed his out rigged service vehicle and trailing hose? What was the repair schedule with parts all over the workshop floor?

Secondly, the bobsled project. Had that been carefully protected and sponsorship passed the next stage of the managements' board meeting?

Thirdly, the invitations to Alfred's pool party and ride on mowing racing, which would be handed out at the pass meeting that night.

Later that evening, Alfred spoke first, once the welcome back to work and safety issues with job front formalities had been got through.

"I need three volunteers, and ten ride on mower competitors."

Without hesitation, the room went quiet and then one, then two, three, four, five, six. Then the whole room put their hands up. The shouts and commotion had to be quietened by management.

"Let Alfred speak," called the supervisor.

"I only need three volunteers and ten competitors," said Alfred, amazed. "I will place a ballot box out and those whose names begin with a certain letter are in."

Alfred was excelling again. Then there was a scramble to get to the ballot box.

What Alfred had not mentioned was that he had wife or partner residing in Alfred the Great's castle. Margareta would only appear on the higher balcony to wave to supporters who encircled the moat on various occasions. Truth be told, they were only nosey onlookers, but Margareta got a kick at waving to them anyway. A flag would be flying high when she was in residence, unless it got tangled up in the solar panels. In that case it would be the job for Alfred to bare his muscles and climb the roof to untangle the flag once again.

Margareta kept a schedule for Alfred, for his comings and goings. Margareta was the love of his life and his favourite beverage.

Hang on a minute, Alfred only goes to work and comes home to do work around the castle. Is there something we don't know about that is kept under wraps?

Some weeks when turning up for work, Alfred was a nervous wreck. It was either Elspeth had given him a hard time, in those few days he was home, giving him a long list of to-dos, or the neighbours were consistently ringing about their power fluctuations. All Alfred could say was the power turbines were being commissioned and the solar and windmill power genera-tors were on standby. "Please be patient, you will have more than enough power soon."

Between the power generation substation and lines distri-bution on private power lines, twice they had been sabotaged by a competition network. The network operators didn't like competition and the ways around power generation Alfred had meticulously thought of. Also the legal ways around the power legislation had caught the network companies off guard.

And so there we have it. It would take Alfred a few days and a few good hours of sleep to recover, hopefully not in work time.

When Alfred did recover, mid-week his work colleagues be-gan to see something very unusual occur in Alfred's appearance. Alfred's eyes would change colour from brown to blue on sev-eral occasions. Not only that, his hair would change colour at the same time.

There was a worrying aspect to this unusual event and his work colleagues were beginning to think he was dehydrated, or was it a figment of their imagination? Either way, Alfred was im-mediately driven by escort down to the paramedics at the camp and placed under observation till the colour of his eyes and hair changed back to normal. The paramedics had no explanation for this either and told Alfred to take things easy. No stress.

Taking the paramedics at their word, Alfred reported in sick and took the rest of the night off. Alfred didn't tell anyone that he was going back to the camp to watch some of the highlights of last year's Grand Prix racing in Melbourne.

The old Chinese proverb says, *"The journey of a thousand miles begins with one step."*

Alfred recorded his steps every day and he was earning Qantas frequent flyer points at the same time.

Alfred had thought about this long and hard.

That thousand miles beginning with the one step can get him-self and Margareta enough Qantas frequent flyer points to get back to Bavaria.

Alfred had plans to get back to the library historical department to get the blueprints of the underground tunnels for Neuschwanstein castle. From there, the excavations under King Alfred's castle would begin. Alfred also knew he would have to up the stakes in his horse racing and punch out more Alfred crypto currency, without touching his secret gold reserves. Then he would have to pay the contractors to dig and remove the dirt. Alfred would also have to invite them to his pool party and pay them to keep quiet about his secret tunnels.

So this swing on, Alfred would be walking anywhere and everywhere. Even if he couldn't walk, he would attach his phone to the fuel hose reel or give his phone to a colleague who was walking even further. This worked out well, Alfred could clock up one hundred thousand steps a night between four colleagues. They thought he was just emptying his pockets and needed someone to hang onto his phone.

Alfred thought, *The Chinamen that came up with that proverb was right on the mark.* It wasn't too hard to a walk thousand miles with others' help after the first step had been initiated.

Alfred disappeared in the early hours of the morning on the mine site. The generators and servicing had all been done. But no fuel truck. An APB was about to be initiated as Alfred had not picked up any radio acknowledgements. There were two of Alfred's colleagues in the area as well. They had acknowledged the call and would investigate. Radios and transmitting and receiving onsite is very important, especially with mobile plant and heavy equipment operating in the vicinity.

Alfred's last-known position was at the dispatch hut, one of the last generators to fill onsite and maintain. Alfred had given a welcoming hello to the ladies in the dispatch hut control centre, advising of his refuelling and maintenance preparation on their machinery.

Alfred had to get out of there quick as the ladies took it to heart, thinking he had come to work on their personal machinery, which gave them a bit of a smile.

Anyway, getting back to Alfred's disposition. The mechanical equipment was inspected and refuelled, and Alfred was on his way. To where though, we were not sure.

It was the crack of dawn. The sun was about to rise. It was then Alfred had been found outside the explosives hut and there was not just one chair but there were three chairs with three people in attendance watching the sunrise once again. His colleagues had called in, having found Alfred, and had decided to join in for this momentous occasion. Not only was the sun rising but Alfred had brought out his ukulele and was singing to himself when his colleagues found him. Initially they thought Alfred was still suffering from heat stress but when they heard Alfred singing *"Tiptoe through the tulips,"* they knew this might be more than just heat stroke. Giving him water in between his breaks with his singing, they began to check his vital signs. Alfred's eyes and hair had changed colour once more.

Letting him keep strumming that ukulele with a smile on his face, they waited till he ran out of words to sing and he could strum no more and then they said, "Come on, Alfred, home time, sleep time. Time to punch those ZZZ's out."

Alfred was more than happy, as one of his fitter colleagues jumped in with Alfred and drove the fuel cart back to the workshop whilst Alfred was trying to retune his ukulele.

No one knew Alfred had a partial musical talent.

We are now finding out more about Alfred's personal achievements in working ours. It was also acknowledged that Alfred had a very rear case of changing eye and hair colour syndrome. What brought that on would be now under medical investigation. But this did not stop him from his work obligations as he was still considered medically fit, but was asked to keep working on his vocals in his downtime and acknowledge all radio calls.

THE GREAT LEAP FORWARD

You don't have to take a page out of Mao Zedong's book on the Great Leap Forward when it came to Alfred. Alfred had proved himself as the fastest streaker on site.

A world class bobsled designer,
still looking for crew to man it
A currency trader
A historic castle builder and
power reticulation controller
And now a musician in his own
right alongside his fitter
and fuel cart portfolio.

Alfred would go on to lead the pass meetings for the remainder of the night shifts for the swing.

He would point out the dangers of dehydration, what factors lead up to the critical stages, and also the changing colours of eyes and hair that might have been aggravated by dehydration and mental fatigue.

This didn't stop Alfred from planning the pool party and charitable ride on mower race in Alfred the Great's castle grounds.

Through Alfred's leadership qualities, there was a new generation of young achievers coming through the ranks and Alfred also wanted to promote this up front at his pool party.

It would come to pass that all information regarding the castle pool party would be mentioned at every pass meeting on his swing until that momentous day.

Isn't it great? Alfred thought.

Morale was at its highest at work. This was the great leap

forward in Alfred's eyes.

Personal responsibility.

Team effort.

Competitiveness with dedication.

The workshop was a better place with Alfred being the motivator, the inspiration, the designator, and the delegator, not to say everyone on the team didn't have their part to play.

There were also times when Alfred didn't get it always right. There was a phone call this day to one of Alfred's trusted electrical colleagues. Something was very much troubling Alfred. Just when Alfred had worked out the logic of thinking outside the square all those years ago, there was a problem with powering up the outside facilities of his swimming pool in the castle grounds. Alfred had been thinking about this over the last few nights, whilst powering through his workload.

The foundations of the castle were stone blocks, stacked up on each other, weighing tonnes. Alfred thought he had been caught between a rock and a hard place when it came to powering up the pool facilities. No power, no pool party.

There wouldn't be enough time to use his Qantas frequent flyer points to fly to Bavaria and pick up copies of the blueprints from the history department for the underground secret tunnels for Neuschwanstein Castle, and make the modifications below the surface of Alfred's Castle to the hydro lake prior to the pool party. Alfred would have had to organise civil contractors at short notice, go over the plans when home and this could take weeks, months, or a couple of years.

You know what they say. Rome wasn't built in a day. Come to think of it, nor was Alfred's castle.

Alfred had to think whilst he was at work and he had to think fast.

Meanwhile, Margareta was arranging all the caterers, entertainers, security and security checkpoints for the big night or big day. Cannot be too careful with council building inspectors lurking around. They would snap at the opportunity of getting across that drawbridge and infiltrating Alfred the Great's castle to take photos that would be compared to the 1300s building code. Any noncompliance would be a demolition job as threatened. However, tight security would weed out these council spies and throw them into the moat to cool off.

Each ride on mower had to be checked in case cameras were going to be used to breach copyrights of other modified ride on mowers that had been turbo charged. There was a lot to be arranged. Then the pool party would be the grand finale. There was an orchestral ensemble hired to play Handel's water music and oh Danny Boy the pipes, the pipes are calling. Alfred had to think now to make sure the pipes were installed before Danny Boy's pipes were there and hadn't gone missing.

Alfred came up with this brain wave.

"What if I could get hold of a new drilling rig that hadn't made its way to site?"

A one-hundred-millimetre diameter hole drilled horizontally through the lower foundations of the castle, close to the swimming pool but not in the swimming pool.

Drilling rigs on site were used for drilling holes to great depth to lay explosive charges through heavy rock. What would be the difference, rock is rock and this would be horizontal instead of vertical? Alfred had once again come up with this most brilliant plan, but he would have to see management about the use of a drilling rig and operator, or if worse came to worse going, to the company that assembles drilling rigs if he could use a complete as built rig for exhibition use only. A display for Nandi the mining company.

The pipes and power could be run at the same time, the power having its own circuitry back to the substation from the pool and the water directly from pressure from the water turbines to fill the pool.

These thoughts now were written down whilst on the last three nights of night swing.

Alfred would subconsciously dream about these ideas when he went to sleep when coming back to the camp after night shift.

The mind boggles when it comes to Alfred's ideas, Alfred had thought.

"We live in a time where intelligent people are being silenced so that stupid people won't be offended."

The motivation, the thought pattern, the dreams, the great people around him. Alfred had nothing to lose. The only negative thought that he would try and keep to one side was the council building inspectors. They never had building inspectors when they built the original Neuschwanstein castle back in Bavaria in the 1300s and Alfred's castle was built to the exact specifications which the council building inspectors had. Alfred had even taken out a permit for his pool construction. The pool itself had been fabricated in the rock during the construction of Alfred the Great's castle. Alfred wasn't hiding anything; in fact he had been upfront all along. It  was the council inspectors that hadn't taken him seriously and now they were on the back foot. Alfred had refused them access as he now classed them as spies for the council building department.

Now getting back to the drilling rig. Alfred's first port of call was to a drilling rig assembly company in Rocky (Rockhampton). Alfred had been on good terms with most companies in Rocky who supplied mining equipment and this operation would be no different to drilling through hard rock or coal bases on site to drilling through stone which in effect is rock, but this would be horizontally, roughly three hundred meters to within two meters of the base of the pool. A concrete cutter would cut vertically down to where the drill had bored through the rock. This could all be down accurately with a laser and GPS measurements. *Perfect,* Alfred thought.

"We can do all this on my rostered swing off. Piped and powered. Only the neighbours would think we are widening the moat looking at a drilling rig, thinking it was a digger."

Alfred with his friendly operators had come to the rescue on site for boring holes for the sparkie's (electrician's) electrical equipment and he knew how this all worked.

Two nights to go onsite was Alfred's happy thought. This was going to be his Happy Hour, not a party Happy Hour yet.

Ten days to go and counting for the pool party. All the invitations had been replied with ninety percent positive "yes" reply. Word had got right around the mining site from the maintenance workshops, the operators crib hut, the dispatch operators to management who were now sponsoring the party. This was going to be a real festive season celebrating in the medieval times. A drawbridge for entry. The only downfall was security at the gate. The costumes, Elspeth of course, would be registering the guests and calculating how much profit would come in for the night's takings. Then there was the charitable ride on mower race, the grand finale, the commissioning of the pool. This wouldn't have happened in the 1300s as no one would have known what swimsuits or buggie smugglers were. If you don't know what buggie smugglers are, they are a term we use here in Australia for men's swimming briefs and I'll let you imagine what the buggie is. Alfred was a big fan of these as he liked to show off his masculinity.

Now the next day after awakening from his sleep, ready to plan for the evening's work, Alfred had it on his mind to make contact with the company that built the assembled drilling rig and immediately advised what was on his mind.

In an hour's conversation and thrashing out the details, a reply came back to Alfred from the manager.

"We have never done anything like this before on request. You realise as this is a first, we will have to make some recorded footage to keep on file for future requests. Also, you will have to pay for truck transport fees as well as wide load coverage fees for land and transport costs."

Fortunately that week, another bonus for Alfred, his dividends had exceeded more than enough, and his crypto currency had risen considerably as well. Alfred knew it was time to take the crypto out and pay for the driller and drilling operations before the crypto dived.

Smart thinking, Alfred. Alfred could now feel at peace that night as he went to work. There would be more than just a spring in his step as he thought how he negotiated a contract as a private castle owner with a mining supplier.

That night, Alfred forgot about the counting of sheep. He went straight into the pass meeting with exuberance. Alfred had a safety share from home. When asked to speak, Alfred brought up the subject of power restoration and good will between neighbours. Going home on break in a day or so, the electrical contractors had worked around the clock to commission the hydro power station for generating not only Alfred the Great's castle, but the neighbours on the other side of the moat as well. There was the careful reinstallation of the line's network to be supplied from Alfred's power station with the onlooking of Ergon Power engineers in distaste. They were there to find safety breaches they could hang on Alfred as he was the responsible owner of the castle.

They were also upset with Alfred because they didn't get a personal invitation to the pool party.

When Alfred mentioned this in the pass meeting, there was a round of cheering.

"Everyone here now has personal invitations.
Just show your work ID cards."

Then there was another round of cheering.

That night in the workshop and down in the pit, everyone took their job fronts a little more seriously.

The excitement of the pool party and the ride on mower challenge had brought a high quality of morale back to all trades on the work front.

THE INCIDENT

Back to the refuelling. It was during this important fuelling session on site that night, nights before finishing Alfred's tour of duty, that something happened to one of the operators. Yes, an operator parked up his 796 Cat mining truck and then collapsed. An emergency was called on site and everything had to stop. Fortunately, this time Alfred heard the call. He raced back to the workshop. When I mean race, Alfred drove at a leisurely pace.

"An operator has just taken a turn for the worst," he was told. "We have managed to get him out of his cab and down the stairwell. The flying doctors have been called in."

This was around 11:30 p.m. that night.

"But there is no lighting at the airport," someone spoke out.

The flying doctors had requested toilet paper dipped in diesel and then lit as flares all the way down the runway. The pilots could see the runway within thirty nautical miles at night. Everyone thought this was a great idea, especially Alfred. Alfred had stockpiled toilet rolls in case of emergencies and this was an emergency, not one that he had expected.

Alfred, along with the team of tradesmen were the first to race to the scene as he had the refuelling truck and half the amount of toilet rolls. When questioned about the toilet rolls as they had been in short supply at the camp, Alfred immediately responded it was for this very occasion these toilet rolls were required. There were also some enthusiastic members of the mechanical workshop who had given a positive response to be part of this planned toilet roll enlightenment for the emergency response for the flying doctors. One young lad was a fella by the name of Trevor Keen. Yes, he was a good keen man. Just like Alfred, he too had a fascination with hoarding toilet rolls as a fitter mechanic. What is

it between toilet rolls and fitters, as between the two of the them they had enough toilet rolls to light the runway for the RFDS (The Royal Fling Doctor Service)?

So Alfred used ninety percent of his cherished toilet rolls, had a bucket to soak them in diesel, Trevor with a smile on his face gave for the cause his ninety percent of his stashed toilet rolls for the greater good and down the runway they went. They positioned the toilet rolls at three-meter spacings on either side at the same distance not to confuse the pilot of the RFDS since the toilet rolls were lit.

Coming in behind was the gas torch igniter who wanted to remain anonymous. He was a union delegate and didn't want to appear as anyone special.

Whilst everyone on site was down tools for the emergency, the Royal Flying Doctor Pilot that night within thirty nautical miles saw the lit-up runway of flared toilet rolls.

Hang on a minute. Was the pilot radioing in that he was seeing double runways? Surely, he wasn't having double vision.

Alfred got the radio call from his concerned supervisor.

"Alfred, how many toilet rolls did you and Trevor lay out? The RFDS pilot is saying he is seeing two parallel runways."

Alfred had realised Trevor had gone a bit further on his runway dimensions.

"I'll have the fuel cart with flashing light and headlights on the correct runway lighting," Alfred radioed.

There could have been two emergencies that night. The casualty of the young man and the misinterpretation of an improvised runway by the Royal Flying Doctor Service. This would not have gone down well and an investigation on team Alfred would have been initiated.

However, due to Alfred's quick thinking, a disaster was avoided. Their lights shone bright that night. The Royal Flying Doctor Service landed safely, and the patient was transferred from the medic's vehicle to the Royal Flying Doctor aircraft. Everyone was relieved. The cheers went up again for Alfred and his team.

In the operators' hut that night whilst they were all sitting around watching movies due to the emergency evacuation, word got back that Alfred and his team had pulled off this daring attempt to get the Royal Flying Doctor Service in and landed safely. Here to in the operator's crib hut went the cheering.

Now a night before fly out, Alfred and Trevor had carried out one of the most daring operations on site. They both had been forgiven for hoarding so much toilet paper from the camp whilst others went without, as this would prove beneficial in the long run.

But this brings me to my point. Who knows the mind of Alfred, it's a mystery. If it hadn't been for the sacrifice of those in the camp for shortages of toilet rolls and Alfred with his young friend Trevor hoarding those toilet rolls, the outcome could have been more serious.

Alfred and Trevor would go on to win an award for what they and team did that night.

The toilet roll manufacturer got wind of the emergency operation with their toilet rolls and decided to do a full promotion nation-wide on their products.

In the next few months, Alfred, Trevor and the reluctant union delegate were sent two years' supply of toilet rolls to compensate for what they had used from their own personal supply and more as a big thank you for using and promoting their product.

Young Trevor was beginning to earn a name for himself. We will study him in a bit more in depth shortly. But for now the legend of Alfred the Great would move on.

The runway lit up with toilet paper.

You could hear those tyres pound
    as they raced across the ground
and the clatter of the wheels as
    they spun round and round
as he raced into the field that day
    with his fuel card on his chest
his name was Alfred and he drove
    the fastest fuel cart in the west

Now Alfred loved a widow,
    a lady nicknamed Rita, and
she lived in a castle high above
    whilst Alfred was away.
They said she was too good for him
    as she was naughty, proud and shy
but Alfred got his Margareta
    there three times every swing.
They called him Alfred and he drove
    the fastest fuel truck in the west.

Now Alfred had a rival,
    an unusual-looking man.
They called him two-ton Ed
    from Cannington

and he drove a second van
    but Alfred had the
upper hand and knew just what to do.
Expand his running costs
    with his faithful fuel
his Margareta at his very hand.
Alfred, he drove the fastest
    fuel truck in the west.

If there was anything Alfred and Trevor had learnt from this series of events, while some people get caught with their pants down for lack of toilet paper, storing it for emergencies is a matter of survival.

That last night for Alfred on site, he came down with a headache. Not of his own doing of course but his neighbours' doing and secondly, the advanced planning for securing that drilling rig. The pool party was only two weeks away; the plumber and the electrician were waiting for the hole to be drilled through basement block from the substation to the extremities of the pool. Cables and piping had to be run in conjunction and to be sealed so rodents could not get in.

The tradesmen had a time frame, Alfred having paid the initial instalments and agreeing to a separate contract for each of their work.

Trades people were hard to get in the present economic climate. The private contractors on the coast were so busy, just to make an appointment, you had to plan weeks in advance to get their expert advice. So arranging to be there on time to supervise the drilling rig, operator, transport logistics to getting the rig to the edge of the moat without the rig falling in would take precision planning.

The preparations and the learning skills over the years in Alfred's work activities had prepared Alfred for this very moment.

The other dreaded thought for Alfred was the neighbours.

They couldn't understand why they couldn't have a conventional square wall dividing the boundaries of their properties.

Carefully Alfred had to bring in the square peg in the round hole theory.

A round moat with a square wall. A square wall would effectively land up in the moat.

There would have to be a compromise for all neighbours. A meeting would have to be called at a later date, as Alfred could see his moat surrounded by partial round walls dividing the neighbours' properties around his moat. Inviting them to the up-and-coming pool party and signing with them a power contract to supply them power at a discounted rate was one thing, being surrounded by half round walls one hundred and eighty degrees round his moat would be a nightmare for visitors trying to navigate their way to the beach. Alfred could see a weary traveller completely missing the side road and hitting a rounded brick wall. Then the council authorities would have to step in, if they hadn't already, with brick wall permits for boundary fences. Yes, there would have to be compromise. An urgent meeting would have to be planned after the pool party.

This wasn't placed in the too hard basket; this planning was for another day.

Alfred's headache was starting to ease as he now was putting everything into perspective.

It had been an extremely full on seven days for Alfred and Trevor. Yes, how was Trevor managing to recover from the lack of toilet paper, Alfred had forgotten to ask. He too was completely depleted of his reserves and had to get through the following day before he too went on his break.

THE ASS HOLE
NOT THE ARSE HOLE

Alfred had really two main fears surrounding him.

1) Unruly neighbours.

2) Sharks in the water.

Alfred always worked on the principle "to love thy neighbour as thy self." A very strong commandment. But what do you do with a deaf neighbour or neighbours who don't get it right?

Well, sharks in the water. Alfred had only swum at the beach twice in in his life for fear of been taken by a great white or a tiger shark. Come to think of it, Alfred had only gotten up to his knees in salt water, having not ever submerged below a wave. Well, Alfred, your loss and the hungry shark out there somewhere. Alfred had taken it upon himself to manage this shark eating step.

That narrows everything down to loving thy neighbour or neighbours.

Alfred had arrived back at Rocky Airport by air taxi the next morning, straight off a night shift with all his work colleagues. A taxi was awaiting to pick Alfred up and chauffeur him home to the castle. This was the only taxi driver who had a security pass to drive across the drawbridge when it was down into Alfred's castle. Alfred's lovely Margareta couldn't drive or even speak English as she was of Spanish descent with a grudge against the English, a grudge going back centuries when the English sank her great-great-great-grandfather's Spanish Galleon, thinking he was a pirate, and all he was doing was holidaying off the South

American coast with his family. Margareta's great-grandfather survived and she was the offspring of the survivors. They never did find the great-great-great-grandfather or the gold.

Alfred had become friendly with Margareta through an interpreter all those years ago on his European trip and the stopover in Bavaria for his historical castle blueprints. Margareta had been working in a backpackers' hostel in mainstream Bavaria when Alfred had turned up that night, cold, wet, and miserable, with no spring in his step. Alfred's first acknowledgement to Margareta was he needed a room with a bath. She politely thought he needed a bar that smoked cigars and pointed in the direction to two shops down the street. Tired and weary, Alfred wasn't perturbed by Margareta's reply and drew a little picture of a bed and a bath. Alfred then politely asked her name, having drawn another picture of a person representing Alfred holding up a piece of paper with his name on it and encouraged this young lady, having displayed what he meant in names. She smiled and wrote, "Margareta."

Alfred, a little upset by now, said he didn't want a margarita. He wanted to know her name. Fortunately, the manager came through the entrance, pulled out his hand to shake Alfred by the hand, and said, in an Austrian accent, "Welcome."

This is going from bad to worse, Alfred thought. *A Spaniard to a Kraut. I hope I can get some sense from him.*

"Please let me introduce myself, my name is Adolf Gal-land. Please may I introduce my assistant, Margareta."

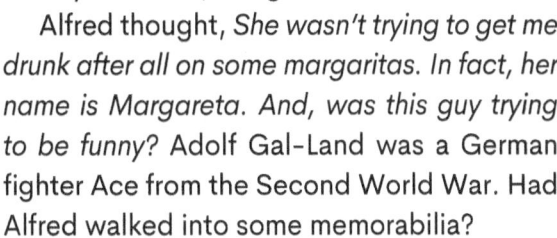

Alfred thought, *She wasn't trying to get me drunk after all on some margaritas. In fact, her name is Margareta. And, was this guy trying to be funny?* Adolf Gal-Land was a German fighter Ace from the Second World War. Had Alfred walked into some memorabilia?

However, Alfred did get a bath and a bed that night. And he did get to greet Margareta. The rest is history. Alfred only came for the history and to get the building plans from the castle's library and Margareta insisted she would come along as well and show Alfred the sites of the country she called her second home, Bavaria. Alfred would get to see a few more sites of Margareta as well and eventually, Margareta didn't want to part with Alfred. Alfred did the right thing and brought Margareta home to Rock Hampton to meet the parents with an interpreter, as she still had a problem with speaking English. Eventually she was persuaded to learn and speak Australian as this had been Margareta's second home and now with the excitement, Australia would be her third home. That's if Alfred wanted her to stay.

And that's how Alfred got to be in the possession of a Margareta and he didn't like coming home to an empty castle and no Paella Valenciana.

Getting back to the neighbours. Alfred had sent circulars to every neighbour's letter box, advising there would be some upgrades on outer perimeters of the castle moat taking place in the next twenty-four to forty-eight hours in preparation for the up-and-coming pool party, which they were all invited to. "Please, we do not want any council initiatives at this stage as we are all in this together," explained Alfred.

"We propose to drill a hole through the lower dimensions of the rock foundations with a specialised drilling machine, roughly one hundred to two hundred and fifty meters in from the outer wall. There may be a little inconvenience with some noise, but I can assure you, it won't be for very long."

With the written affirmation and expecting positive replies from his neighbours, Alfred didn't expect a confused reply from two of his closest elderly neighbours, or maybe he should have.

The reply was as follows:

"We take offence to your letter dated on the 20th May 2022 regarding, in your terms, calling us arse holes, and that you would be personally drilling through our lower foundations."

There seemed to be some confusion "the drilling 'a' hole" through the lower rock foundations of the castle and not their personal foundations.

Alfred would of course see his neighbours immediately, to clear up the matter, as his confirmed drilling rig was arriving at 8.00 a.m. sharp the following morning.

Alfred now had this sense of urgency to see his neighbours, the closest on either side of his drawbridge, and he was determined to take a food hamper with him to soothe the neighbours' concerns of their misinterpretation of Alfred calling them an arse hole.

Alfred would remind them too, that they were invited to his pool party in the weeks to come. This hopefully would be the ice breaker.

So with the immediate concern on Alfred's mind, Alfred promptly contacted both neighbours on either side of his drawbridge early the following morning before the drilling rig would arrive by road transport.

The following morning, the morning after Alfred had arrived home from the long week on the mine site still in a state of weariness, the drawbridge was lowered. Alfred was on horseback as though he was a knight in shining armour and, with a kiss from his beloved Margareta, set forth with papers and pictures in his man bag to give the neighbours a heads up.

This looked impressive although the neighbours were only twenty meters away on either side of the moat.

Alfred also advised the two young fellas fishing in his moat as he passed by.

"There are only crocodiles down there," he said as he pointed to the "Beware of Crocodiles" and "Fish at your Own Risk" signs.

Three council building inspectors had fallen into the moat having been picked up by security as so-called guests trying to infiltrate the castle premises. They had never been seen since. A wallet and finger were found in days to come but nothing more. The local police had called for an investigation into the suspicious circumstances, but there had been no real witnesses as it had been dark on both nights the men had disappeared.

Alfred had dismounted his horse, having tied it to the neighbour's tree.

KNOCK, KNOCK, KNOCK on the solid oak door.

Alfred had been on good terms with his neighbours, although he had only met them once. A lovely old retired couple whose parents had come from Europe, having been displaced in the USA before a World War II, and had them come to Australia to start a new life with. A then young son Albert Einstein junior and his sister Ingrid.

The door opened and a briskly elderly gentlemen carefully opened the door.

"Good morning, Albert, may I have a word with you about your concerns with your upcoming brick wall?" asked Alfred graciously.

Alfred of course relied on his diplomacy with all his neighbours. To upset them would be a backwards step. To listen to their grievances and formulating a plan that both parties would agree to was in both party's interests.

"Come in, we have been expecting you," said the young Albert, although he was young but the junior to his father Albert Einstein senior.

The biggest thing on Albert's mind was discussing the "law of relativity" to the problem that lay before them. This was emphasised at some considerable depth by his late father and mentor growing up.

With some discussion and white board activity, Alfred was beginning to see the relevance of the Relativity Theory coming into the equation for both sides of the neighbour's brick wall.

Alfred had drawn up possible modules for Albert and his wife to see. The variances ranged from a high brick wall with rounded edges to a brick wall with glass interior, all to still keep their privacy, to an imaginary brick wall that could be described in detail but wouldn't exist.

When it came to the law of relativity, which was the energy to put the brick wall up, Energy (E) equals mass (m) times the speed of light (c) squared (2) or E= mc2.

The secret of the equation revealed that mass and energy are different forms of something and this has frustrated scientists for centuries.

But Alfred, he got it. The energy required to put the brick walls up, with mass of its weight and the speed of light. This would have to be done in daylight hours. Squared, the wall had to be squared off.

Alfred was a fitter mechanic by trade and always made things fit squarely. Although he didn't always get it right.

Alfred had conquered the concerns of his neighbours and he would leave the premises with a load off his chest. A victory!

Alfred now had not only understood Einstein's law on relativity, it was there in plain English and Albert Einstein senior was German.

Alfred said to the Einsteins, "Here is a little something for you and your lovely wife, in appreciation for us coming to an agreement. A token from the castle's establishment."

It was a food hamper specially chosen by Margareta.

As Alfred was leaving to go to the neighbour on the other side of the drawbridge, Albert junior called out, "Please don't forget the law of relativity for future references."

"I won't," replied Alfred. "And please accept my invitation to the pool party."

"I won't," replied Albert junior. "By the way, when is it?"

"Check your mailbox," Alfred called back.

The neighbour on the other side of the drawbridge would be then contacted by appointment and his concerns would be laid to rest by the simple formula Albert junior had given him. The law of relativity.

THE DRILLING RIG

Riding his stallion that had been leased back to the castle that morning and then placing it in the handler's care, Alfred was waiting for the phone call from the drilling rig company. Alfred would be overseeing the truck and trailer carrying the rig to site, being set up at the foot of the moat—not at the foot of the moat but within a two-meter radius from the foot of the moat, as it had been raining considerably in the area. A potential cave in with a drilling rig sitting tail up in the moat wouldn't do much for Alfred's reputation for attention to detail.

Written into the insurance contract was nothing about a potential moat wall collapse, only sinking of a drilling rig due to uneven ground or soft ground due to water contamination.

All this was only on the first day home after a night shift. Alfred was reminded of the saying, "The show's not over till the fat lady sings."

Who was the fat lady? Alfred thought. *She must have been a classic.*

But this was a show to be carried out and not a no show, if you know what I mean.

Planning, operators, timing, road transport, site preparation, neighbours and now the weather.

This was manageable in Alfred's eyes. The phone call did come from the drilling company. Everything was in order with the land transport. A wide load and steering of the truck and trailer transport on the heavy bypass road enroute to Alfred's castle.

Alfred was in town on his four-wheeler with flashing lights to escort the truck and trailer to his real estate. Having signed road transport documents and having paid a fee in advance, the police were willing to help with inconvenience to the public road as the drilling rig on the trailer passed through.

Time was of the essence now as Alfred had only a matter of days, six days to be exact, for the hole to be bored through castle foundations for powering and plumbing the pool. The actual pool layout had been laid with modelling in the initial construction, a slight modification to the original plans. I'm sure the Roman bath houses in their establishments had a similar concept.

Alfred could do with a hand. Being the project engineer, the administrator, the production manager, and the HR officer for safety was a big ask, even if it was Alfred's castle establishment. The workers had gone on strike for lesser claims than what Alfred was trying to achieve. But hang on a minute, how could Alfred go on strike when there was only one of him?

Time to call in for reinforcements. This would be done at the drill fitter's yard.

With a phone call to Ikav, a tall robust Papua New Guinean national with brute strength and a fitter by trade, Alfred would ask at short notice if he could be a part of the engineering team to ensure everything went smoothly at one end of the hole boring tunnel.

This is the conversation.

"Ikav, I have a slight need of your services."

"What for?" came Ikav's reply.

"I've dug myself into a deep hole, not the pool hole, Ikav, but trying to manage every front of finishing this swimming pool. Can you spare a couple of days just to get the hole drilled with this rig?"

"You're out of Rocky. I'm in Townsville, eight hundred kilometres, big distance, Alfred," said Ikav.

"We can come together with some arrangements for the cost of flight down here and can fly back to the mine site from here on the mining charter back to work," replied Alfred.

Alfred of course had to give an incentive. What could that be? A free holiday to the castle and visiting site for family once a year? Or maybe free access to the new aquatic pool and centre Alfred was building? A lifetime pass?

Nandi, the original sponsor of the pool party, had fallen through and the company Care Free had agreed to take over the original sponsorship. *That's a relief*, thought Alfred as they were only days away from the big event and the invitations had been sent, even to the remaining council inspectors. They were down to one now who had agreed to incorporate the original blueprint castle plan into the Queensland building code. He was invited in good faith.

"I'll come," replied Ikav. "On two conditions: First, you don't let any of those crocodiles around me. Second, I take a share in the profits from the new aquatic centre with passes for myself and family."

Without thinking about the implications, this was a done deal on Alfred's behalf.

The implication was Margareta. Since she couldn't speak a word of English and her interpreter was not always available due to family issues, she would get upset thinking Ikav was another one of those spies coming to infiltrate the premises.

Alfred would deal with that later. In the meantime, it was done.

"Done," said Alfred. "I'll get you on the Qantas link flight this afternoon and pick you up from the rocky airport early this evening, Ikav."

And so it was agreed.

A happy Alfred, another negotiated deal. Happy neighbours, happy work colleague.

Alfred was now riding his chariot of four wheels, fired up in front of the truck and semi-trailer out of the drilling rig yard. Alfred rode that four-wheeler chariot with flashing lights and the siren running fifty meters in front of the semi-trailer so he wouldn't get run over.

The back streets to the heavy truck bypass road were cleared, although missing a few scary corners. This was now a full-on operation for Alfred. Estimated elapsed time from departure to destination is two hours exactly.

The drilling would begin early afternoon. Ikav would arrive early evening, as by then the one-hundred-millimetre diameter hole would only be a quarter of the way through. The most significant part of Ikav turning up would be himself at the other end of the hole making sure the drill didn't go through the base of the pool complex and through the incoming sewer pipe. Terrible combination, a Pooh pool.

The drill was well on the way. 8 a.m. came and went. 9 a.m. came and went. 10 a.m., the rig turned up outside the castle estate.

Alfred had marked out the hole to drill in the foundations using GPS. Alfred had seen this work very successfully underground between levels when cables had to be run. Thinking, *If the sparkies can do it, surely it cannot be TOO hard.*

What Alfred hadn't considered or forgotten about was the big septic tank to the right side of the pool, ten meters away. The GPS had picked up the Pooh Pond pool instead of the shell of the swimming pool.

The drilling rig was set up in position, its tracks firmly embedded in the ground and not sinking.

Explaining to the drilling operator that the hole had to be straight on the mark, horizontally with no incline or decline drilling, Alfred gave the instructions to the drilling operator to drill.

Matter of fact, the operator was the mining site drilling operator, and a very experienced drilling operator at that, happy enough to make a few dollars on the side to help Alfred out.

There was no limit to Alfred's friends, they came from far and wide as you see. But his hole could get a little messy as you can see the mark is in the wrong place.

Gratitude is the most powerful tool.
No matter what's going on around you,
every day take a moment to reflect on everything
you have to be grateful for.

This was Alfred. Things could get a bit messy but he was grateful to his friends and things around him. Alfred was humble, and most of all, Alfred was funny.

Laughter is medicine and Alfred knew it.

Having now started the drilling operations into the stone foundation, the neighbours congregating around the barricade exclusion zone to see what was happening, the drilling was underway. A three drill through heavy rock initially had been planned as Ikav had to be picked up from the local Rocky airport.

Ikav had just landed in Rocky (Rockhampton), Queensland. There waiting on time for Ikav was Alfred. Alfred greeted Ikav and grabbed his luggage. His shuttle car was waiting, complete with driver.

"Come, Ikav, we got work to do," called out Alfred. "We can have this done in a day or so."

"No problem," said Ikav, rubbing his head and thinking, *What have I let myself in for?* Working straight away was not Ikav's idea of fun, however, Ikav was here to do a job to help Alfred and he would do it properly.

The castle shuttle left the airport and within the space of half an hour, the view of Alfred the Great's castle and the drilling machine were in view. Not only was the drilling machine and the castle in view but the neighbours and locals had been out in force to see what the loud noise was all about.

Ikav was still scratching his head a little as the drawbridge was down and the shuttle entered the castle. Ikav had never been inside a castle before, especially the size of this magnitude.

Ikav was amazed at the magnificence and the prestige of such a place.

"Alfred, I thought you were having me on when you said you had built a castle. How long did it take you to build this massive structure?" asked Ikav.

"Ikav, I'll tell you later. Let's just get this hole drilled and then you can ask all the questions you want. Will take you on a guided tour then," Alfred called out.

The drilling rig was still running. The driller had stopped for a bit to make sure Alfred was happy at the progress. Just as well the driller did stop, as what was to come could have been a disaster if it hadn't been for Ikav's quick thinking.

Alfred had given Ikav GPS positions from the outside to the inside. Ikav had studied the pool lay out and the outside hole position. Looking at the plan layout, the sewage tank layout, Ikav could see a problem straight away.

"Stop!" called Ikav. "You're heading straight for the sewage tank."

"What?" called Alfred.

"Whoever set these GPS coordinates up has missed the mark on both sides."

Alfred couldn't believe it, and had to admit to Ikav, he had a bit to do with it.

"These measurements are back to front," said Ikav.

Without a thought, Alfred had just remembered he was dyslexic. All those years of skillfully working around being dyslexic had now come to light.

"Okay, I admit it, Ikav. I set those GPS coordinates up and I'm dyslexic," said Alfred.

"No problem," said Ikav. "We will just reverse the coordinates, so they don't go through the pool or the tank."

Then they had a great laugh.

Ha ha ha.

It was nearing sunset now, tomorrow was another day. Alfred felt sure with the help of Ikav, they could fix the problem tomorrow with a new hole, this time in the right position. A job now that would take the required two days. The driller and drilling rig had been hired for three days and was still well inside Alfred's budget.

Margareta had prepared a Spanish banquet for all the guests and there was only two. Ikav and Alfred.

Well, the food could last for a few days after the banquet. Nothing would go to waste. Ikav had a good appetite and with the help of Alfred, they could polish off half of what Margareta had prepared and some for breakfast.

Margareta didn't have an interpreter that night, so Ikav thought he would create some small talk.

"Buenas noches, Margareta."

"Buenas noches para una mujer a un hombre," came the reply, as Margareta smiled.

Ikav hadn't a clue what she just said. He only knew these words and greetings.

Buenas noches. Good evening.

Buenos dias. Good day.

Gracias. Thank you.

Señor. Mr.

Señora. Mrs.

That was Ikav's limit in Spanish. When Margareta didn't get a reply from Ikav, she thought he was rude and stormed off. The truth was Ikav didn't understand a word she was saying.

Ikav was a little surprised.

"It's okay, Ikav," said Alfred. "She does that to me as well and eventually she comes back all lovey dovey 'cause she wants something."

Ikav just sat back and smiled his big smile.

"Now tell me, Alfred, how long did it take you to build this castle, and how did you finance this?" asked Ikav. "I thought you were joking when you kept mentioning this to me at work."

"The truth is, Ikav, I went to the bank and showed the bank manager the castle blue prints, asking for a loan in the vicinity of twenty million dollars. Also outlining the business venture inside the castle. I mentioned to you the aquatic centre and the rooms with suites to be hired out to anyone who wanted to pay top dollar."

"And what happened?" asked Ikav.

"The bank manager fell out of his chair laughing; he couldn't contain himself. The only advice he could give me was this: 'There is a toy store down the road, perhaps there is a model castle you could buy and outlay on your property.'"

"And he continued to laugh as I walked out," said Alfred. "It didn't stop me, in fact, it made me more determined. The guy was an idiot, full of himself."

"Then I went to the council building inspectors' department, gave them a copy of the original blueprints of the historical castle I had proposed to build."

"What happened then?" asked Ikav.

"The senior building inspector didn't take me seriously either. I could see in his face that he too was trying to contain his laughter," said Alfred.

"So what happened next, with eyes wide open?" asked Ikav.

"I took the matters into my own hands. I figured, if I built the moat first, the only people in across the bridge would be only those who had business on the castle side of the moat."

"So where did the finance and the builders come from, Alfred?" asked Ikav.

"Remember I told you at work about horse racing and crypto currency," replied Alfred. "I found a way to bet on the winners and losers and like the gambling man, every hand's a winner. You just got to know which cards to keep."

"And what about the crypto?" asked Ikav.

"That exploded," said Alfred. "The moment that coin was in circulation, it had unlimited potential."

"What coin?" asked Ikav.

"The invisible coin with my head on both sides," said Alfred. "The one I was discussing at work. Within weeks of its launching, the money came flowing in."

"So why did you go to this bank?" asked Ikav.

"I just wanted to test the waters, not my moat waters but their mentality," replied Alfred. "And sure enough, small things amuse small minds."

"I tell people the formation of the project took about five

years. In reality, with the moat and foundations, from the very beginning, about ten years," said Alfred.

"Remember," said Alfred, "always think on the bright side of life, de dum, dedum dedum dedum dedum. Oh, by the way, I didn't have trouble getting the stone masons, they appeared out of the woodwork."

"Funny, bro."

"Alfred, that's incredible," said Ikav. "Can you show me the layout after we have eaten?"

"Sure," replied Alfred. "Just to add fuel to the fire, when the council started taking me seriously, it was too late. The building inspectors could not get access across the drawbridge. They tried infiltrating as guests, but security removed them. The crocs in the moat made a meal of them in the dark. There were no witnesses as it was dark. We didn't know what happened to them."

The bank manager eventually was made redundant, as the banks were restructuring. Covid hit and Alfred's castle and all who inhabited it were safe.

So the story now of Alfred's castle would live in the hearts of people forever. Especially Ikav, and maybe Trevor Keen if he got over the toilet roll issue back at camp.

Remember Alfred had to live up to his reputation. The pool party and even the tickets on site were all spoken for.

Alfred and Ikav would sleep well that night after Ikav was taken on a two-hour tour of the castle layout. He was very impressed. Alfred had taken on this quest to secure himself in from the outside world when he needed to be. *Right on, bro,* Ikav thought. *This being on the coast as well, a good family retreat.*

Alfred had conquered, he had a dream.
Alfred had a dream, a fantasy,
to help him through, to reality,
and his destination makes him place a smile,
pushin' through the darkness, at one hundred miles.

Alfred had a dream with a song to sing
to help him cope with anything.
If you see him wonder with a fairy tale
he can make the future, even if he fails.

Alfred had a dream. His voice was improving all the time after those early morning sunrises with his ukulele and his team of three mining colleague supporters. As the sun rose at the crack of dawn, so did Alfred at 5.30 a.m. With a gentle nudge, Ikav was awakened as well.

"Breakfast has been made," Alfred said, paging Ikav on the intercom.

Margareta had waited for Alfred and Ikav, preparing chocolate con churros, soletillas and melindros with pincho de tortilla. Alfred and Ikav hadn't a clue what it was but it sure looked good to start the morning off. Cat pooh coffee to wash it all down with. Yes, cat pooh coffee, a delicacy. Alfred and Ikav didn't know that, thinking it was a flavoured coffee. This was Margareta's treat for the morning.

The drilling for the morning would start around 7.30 a.m. so as not to upset Alfred's delicate neighbours. The plan was in place to drill the utilities hole all that day with no hassles.

So the driller along with the drilling machine and the noise it made would commence under Alfred's direction and Ikav's. Supervision to line the hole up right. If the hole bore went wrong, it would be more than Cat Pooh coffee, they'd all be in the Pooh.

"Gentlemen, are we ready?" Alfred called out.

Hank was getting the drilling rig hydraulics warmed up and then he would proceed with moving the arms with the drills mounted and install the new GPS coordinates.

"Ikav, you take the lead inside the castle on the two way," yelled Alfred over the drilling rig noise.

Ikav thought Alfred said to go and read in the castle, thinking that was a funny response.

Grabbing the two-way walking across the drawbridge into the castle grounds, Ikav did a radio check.

"Radio check, how do you read, Alfred?" called Ikav.

"Read you loud and clear, Ikav," replied Alfred.

"Just confirming you want me to read inside the castle, Alfred?"

"No," came the response from Alfred. "I want you to lead."

"Alrighty," replied Ikav.

The drilling operator was now in place to run the drill through the rock foundation.

"Let the drilling commence," called Alfred, a little nervous.

The rock had been blasted out of a quarry and shaped by stone masons. You could say another chip off the old block. These craftsmen had been hard to find. It was only by Alfred's ingenuity on Facebook and social media that he received a reply for the "stone masons wanted" advertisement. The average age was around ninety-three years and between them, they had three hundred and seventy-two years of experience in their craft, just four hundred years short of the time the original Neuschwanstein castle was built if you take their years as well into account.

The four old men had a contracting business going, in which none of the families wanted to take on. So as dying craft, the four old men would take their ancient skills to the grave. To Alfred, it didn't seem that long at all and he wanted to get in first to get the castle built.

So with a contract in place, the deed was signed and with smiles from four men with no teeth, they were certain this would be their last contract before they would wind up the business and officially retire on the proceeds of the fruits of their labour. They were happy, Alfred was happy.

Also in the contract, there was a note written in small print, "Any extras are not included in the contract price and would be payable on completion."

Alfred had somehow overlooked this as he didn't have a magnifying glass.

The drilling began. As the hole was being bored, water lubricant was being pumped in with the drill head. The driller had brought some extension attachments just in case, as the hole was around thirty to forty meters of solid rock. The main power systems run in the castle were run in ducting with false fabricated walls and ceiling spaces if you are wondering. The walling blended into the castle outlay.

The rock was that hard, they estimated an hour for each meter of drilling with the diamond tip drill. When they use the phrase "it's as hard as rock," it literally was hard rock and hard going.

Alfred just stood and watched and yelled into his two to Ikav, "It's coming."

Only the first meter had been drilled. There was another twenty-nine or so meters to drill.

As the sun rose, so did the neighbours, Albert on one side and Thomas on the other. Come to think of it, Albert Einstein was the creator of the law of relativity. Alfred had learnt about it putting into practice and younger Thomas Edison had experimented with electricity. Both men had benefited Alfred's cause and the cause of many other families in the area.

Closing his eyes for a minute, Alfred reflected that life was good.

Two hours into the operations, two meters had been drilled. Then three meters, then ten, then twelve, they may have to work into the night.

Alfred in the contract had asked for two shifts, day and night. By 8 p.m., a new driller had arrived, fresh and keen to keep working through the night.

The neighbours and Margareta had brought out refreshments for the well-deserved breaks for all three men. It was then Alfred found out that this particular rig was going to be used in a demolition after this job. It wasn't a new rig as thought but an overhauled forty-year rig with a paint job.

Alfred was paying top dollar for something old and decrepit. No wonder the drilling was taking so long.

But Alfred had a plan. Alfred always has a plan. Not sure what. But watch this space.

Half a rig at half the cost. Seems fair. The driller didn't care as he was still getting paid his agreed hourly rate according to his contract.

Alfred would wait until the hole was completed and the drilling rig returned and revalidate the contract on his terms, as a deposit was paid and the terms of complete payment on completion of job.

Alfred had looked up on the internet on his lunch break a 1975 contract agreement for this particular rig and he would back date the cost to forty-seven years ago.

In the original contract it said new equipment, new drill at today's hiring cost. There might have been a couple of things new inside but only a paint job outside done in recent weeks. This could be challenged, old equipment at old prices. This worked well in Alfred's favour as now, if he went over the time limit quoted in the contract price, he would still be ahead on old contract prices and he may even get a refund. The drill hiring company could be challenged on this as a technical issue.

Never thought about that, Alfred, good thinking. We can just about add up a new list of fast achievements in Alfred's favour. Alfred's not just a dreamer but a realist.

After eighteen hours of drilling and a watchful eye, the drill hit something in the core of the rock.

"Ikav, got a copy," called Alfred.

"Reading you clear," came the reply from Ikav.

"We seem to have hit something in the rock, about eighteen meters in. Did you hear anything, Ikav?" Alfred asked.

"Just a crunch and a squeal," came the reply from Ikav.

There was no reinforcing in the rock as this wasn't concrete slabs. They would have to get ahold of the stone masons and see where this portion of rock came from. They were over halfway now and the end was in sight.

The stone mason company was contacted with a follow up in the next hour. The old men, all three of them, came to greet Alfred, smiling with their no teeth smile.

"What seems to be the problem, young Alfred?" one of the men called out.

This was Gerry.

"We've hit something in the stone and not sure what it is. Could you enlighten us where the stone came from and what might be in it?" asked Alfred.

The three old men got together chatting and within a few minutes came to a conclusion.

"The bottom foundation stones of your castle were cut from an old prison buried years ago. We think it might be a collection of skeletons, as the deceased were buried under the stone, according to records of two hundred years ago. We looked at this area before we cut it and were assured by the record office, we were clear of any contaminants," said Gerry. "You should be okay to keep drilling. You will break through that crusty part quite quickly."

Skeletons, thought Alfred. He didn't want skeletons hiding in his closet. The hole bore must go on. It was now or never. The skeletons must be bored through. Fortunately they were not indigenous skeletons if it had been a jail two hundred years ago or else it would be there and then all drilling operations would have had to cease. Instead, there would be an investigation with historians and geologists looking for artefacts. Alfred just shivered for a minute; it could have been worse. Then Alfred called out to the driller, "The show must go on. Pump that water through and keep drilling. Ikav, you copy?"

"Loud and clear, Alfred."

"We are drilling again. Twelve meters to go. Keep an eye out for the drill."

"Copy," said Ikav.

The drill eventually pummelled through to twenty-five, and on the twenty-ninth meter, a call came over the two way from Ikav.

"The hole is nearly through," called Ikav. "Go carefully."

This was great news. Alfred was just about to jump up in the air with excitement, when one of the old stone masons suddenly passed away.

The hole was through and a great statesman of the mason fraternity had gone to be stone mason in the sky.

Gerry, quickly with his colleague and the corpse said their goodbyes as they would have to take the body of their deceased colleague to the undertakers and a death certificate pronounced dead on arrival.

This surely would be their last greatest achievement, Alfred the Great's castle, their names engraved on the entrance of the castle forever. This too would be celebrated, maybe not at the pool party, but later at a special ceremony if the other two old gents were still around.

The stone masons were also in line to win an award for completion of the castle over the ten-to-fifteen-year period. You could say the complete product as castle of the year.

The hole was complete after a thirty-hour hole bore. The electrician and plumber could now be called in. The neighbours were satisfied the noise level was not above eighty-five decibels. But because they were fairly deaf, they wouldn't have noticed anyways if the noise level was above eighty-five decibels.

Alfred was elated, Ikav was intrigued, Margareta was nowhere to be seen.

The drilling machine was loaded back onto the trailer and was sent on its way back to the drilling company. Alfred had the dispute to settle, as the hi-rage was misleading and a breach of the commerce act. He could in effect be in pocket not out of pocket. That was tomorrow.

A celebration was in order. Alfred and Ikav could go back to work knowing the hardest part of tackling the pool problem was over.

Hang on a minute, that was only day three of Alfred and Ikav's week off. They had four days left and Alfred was ahead of schedule. There was a funeral to attend for the deceased stone mason Jimmy Jones. A nice old fella in Alfred's eyes. It was the least Alfred and Ikav could do to attend.

Would Ikav want to stay another three days after the funeral or go home to do whatever he intended to do in the first place before Alfred interrupted him at short notice?

Ikav made the decision to go home. He needed those few days with his family. So it was arranged the next day Ikav would fly back to Townsville on the Qantas flight to see his family and then be ready for work to fly out in three days. Ikav promised to fly back for the pool party on the 22nd of May.

In those long two days, Alfred developed a nervous twitch. This only came on when Alfred was extremely tired. Seeing her hubby in a nervous twitching frame of mind, Margareta immediately brought Alfred up to his favourite bathtub in the castle and had the hot water running. As Alfred de-robed and lay in the bath, Margareta began to rub his shoulders and sing to him in Spanish. Nearly falling asleep and sliding down the bath, Alfred was quickly revitalised when the water level started tickling his nose. He was submerging. With quick thinking Alfred jumped up out of the bath, dried himself, put on a fresh set of clothes, and went looking for Ikav. It was Ikav's last night at the castle and Alfred wanted to show him a bit more of the castle estate and what hidden secrets lay above and below the castle.

Alfred also wanted to show off his red beacon on top of the highest point of the castle.

"This, my friend, is an obstruction light, indicating highest point to all air traffic on the direct approach path to Rockhampton airport." It was flashing intermittently at night also could be picked up on dark cloudy days.

"Alfred, you have thought of everything."

"Not quite, I had a visit from the Australian civil aviation authority. They didn't recommend it, they insisted the height of the castle was well over three hundred meters."

"How many secret passages do you have, Alfred?" asked Ikav.

"Every second room has a secret passage and also in the halls and dining room. If you have a problem with your guests, the only way is out, and locked out," said Alfred.

"Ha ha." Ikav laughed, having seen the high lights of the castle and the stunning views of the coastline.

"Well," said Alfred. "I think I'm going to retire to bed."

"Me too," Ikav said. "Big day tomorrow with Jimmy's funeral and flying home."

After a peaceful sleep, Alfred was up at the crack of dawn. Not uncommon for Alfred as he usually sings with his ukulele and mining colleagues. This time Margareta had fixed a Spanish-style breakfast for Alfred and Ikav.

pincho de tortilla
croissant de almendra
fresh orange juice and coffee
with a welcome greeting to Margareta from Ikav.

"*Buenos dias*, Margareta," said Ikav.

He only knew how to say good morning and good evening, which is buenos noches, as well as thank you, gracias. That was Ikav's limit.

When he made his reply, Margareta thought he could speak her native tongue. "*Buenos dias, señor Ikav, como estas esta mañana?*"

When Margareta didn't get a reply from Ikav, just a stunned look, she stormed off.

"What was that all about?" said Ikav.

"She thought you were fluent in Spanish and wanted to have a conversation with you as her interpreter wasn't here. She thinks you are very rude for not replying," said Alfred.

"I only know how to say three things in Spanish: good morning, good evening, and thank you," said Ikav.

"I know," said Alfred. "She does that to me as well. Margareta will get over it. She always comes back lovey dovey when she wants," said Alfred.

Finishing breakfast, preparations were being made to attend Jimmy Jones' funeral. It would be a gathering of just a few people. Roughly five, including the minister. Most of Jimmy's friends and relations had passed on years ago. But the song always on their minds kept coming back.

Now Jimmy was only ninety-three, he didn't want to die.
He's gone to make those stone blocks
and deliveries in the skies
where the customers are angels
and ferocious dogs are banned.
A stone mason's life is full of fun
in that fairy stone mason's land.
But strange things happened on that very night.
Was it the trees a rustling
or the hinges on the gate
or Jimmy's ghostly stone plate rattling to aggravate?
They won't forget Jimmy
as he was the fastest stone man in the west.

Alfred and Ikav were now on their way to the service. Ikav had packed all his gear as straight after he was catching the Qantas link flight back to Townsville.

The driver of Alfred's favourite shuttle service had been cleared across the drawbridge and parked outside the main entrance pick up point of Alfred's castle, awaiting his guests.

Alfred and Ikav, saying goodbye to Margareta for the duration, saw the car parked through the arched window and opened the heavy entrance door.

The driver had immediately called to Alfred and opened the luggage door and car door.

"Welcome, Mr. Norris, so pleased to be of service."

As Alfred and Ikav slid into the back seat of the shuttle, the conversation started up about Jimmy and the stone masons. *Sounds like a rock band*, Alfred thought.

Leaving the castle grounds and arriving at the small church, Alfred and Ikav entered through the front door of the church and were ushered to their seats. The coffin lay there. Jimmy's photo with toothless smile lay on top. The brotherhood—all two stone masons with Alfred and Ikav—were assembled in front of the coffin. The minister asked if anyone wanted to give the eulogy. Before the stone masons Gerry and Hector could get up, Alfred said, "I will."

"Let's face it," Alfred said. "Jimmy was pretty choosy when he came to picking his friends. I'm surprised some of you made the cut. You can pick your friends but you cannot pick your relations. Jimmy, the party you planned you never made it to. I know they will give you a better party up there, old friend."

With that, Alfred sat down. The minister said a few words, and Jimmy's favourite hymns were played.

"There will be a few refreshments following the service in the back of the church. Jimmy has made sure of that, if you would care to join us."

All five persons including Alfred and Ikav walked briskly to where the refreshment venue was.

Ikav had only a short time before he had to catch the flight back to Townsville, so he made the most of an early lunch whilst he was there. He knew Jimmy would be smiling although he had only met him once, and that was the day he passed away.

Alfred had been in a thinking mood once again after the service. And that was plain to see by Ikav.

"Alfred, old son," said Ikav, "what's on your mind?"

"I've been thinking," said Alfred.

"Oh boy, here it comes."

"The shuttle is outside, got to get you to the airport and then taken home to mark out the grounds for the race in two weeks."

"Well, I got my last bite here," said Ikav. "Let's go."
The door once again was opened for the two men and the pleasantries exchanged.

"To the airport, Rupert," called Alfred.

"Yes sir," replied Rupert.

The drive would only last twenty minutes, having green traffic lights all the way to the Qantas departures. The shuttle bus stopped. Ikav got out with his one piece of carry on. Alfred shook Ikav's hand and said his thank yous.

"Till we meet again, old friend," said Alfred.

Hang on a minute, Alfred would be seeing Ikav at work in two days.

"Alfred, haven't you forgotten something?" said Ikav.

"And what's that, Ikav?"

"I'll see you in two days," said Ikav.

"Slipped my mind."

Having dropped Ikav off, it was time to head back to the castle. Awaiting at the moat would be some German tourists. That's right, tourists not terrorists.

As the van rolled up, a young German man quickly spoke up as Alfred rolled the window down.

"Guten tag, ich frage mich nur, wer der besitzer ist und ob sie mich in kontakt mitnehmen konnten."

In English. "Good afternoon, just wondering who the owner is and if you could put me in contact with him."

"Guten tag, der bersitzer ist nicht hier, komm in zwie wochen nach einer besonderen eröffnungsfeier zurück."

In English. "Good afternoon, the owner is not here. Come back in two weeks after a special opening ceremony."

Alfred advised the German tourists that there was a camp down the road near the beach.

The young German had recognised the castle as a copy of a historical castle in Bavaria and was fascinated, commenting on it to Alfred.

Alfred couldn't believe he had said that all in German, as he was a little rusty. Adolph Gal-Land had really done a good job on helping him with his German in Bavaria, as Alfred never forgot it or him as a matter of fact. The odd phone call from Bavaria would come in every now and again in a conference call.

As the drawbridge was now down and the shuttle van was across, Alfred had another ingenious thought.

"Wait, driver," said Alfred. "Turn the shuttle around. We are going to find those German backpackers."

Alfred had this thought right. They were German, the castle had a German background, they knew the castle that his was modelled off in Bavaria. A job offer could be on the cards for the four Germans. Margareta could surely use a hand when Alfred was away working. Working visas would still be required although Alfred has his own kingdom and no one outside could come in to check without being invited in.

And so the shuttle van raced back across the drawbridge to find those young Germans and as it would happen, a job offer was confirmed for the duration of their working visas, on the condition they could live in and come and go as they pleased.

One main condition was insisted on by Alfred. No parties. Happy Hours were permitted as long as the noise was kept down. This was agreed. That's how Alfred got his staff members established, just an accident outside the boundaries of the castle when four German tourists set their sights to find the owner of the newly named Alfred the Great's castle.

The last but not least of things to do the following day was the markings on the lawn for the ride on race in two weeks. This would be a novelty for the young Germans and something to write home about. The pool as well had been painted the colour purple, Alfred's favourite colour, and would be lit up into the night sky at night with the pool lights. The Australian Civil Aviation Safety office would probably now use Alfred's castle as a way point for approaches into Rockhampton airport. How about that, a danger beacon that was red at the highest point on the castle and his lit-up swimming pool at night. No pilot should ever miss the approach into Rockhampton airport again.

Alfred is more than man of the hour. Logistically, Alfred has increased the tourism in the area, although people cannot get across the drawbridge into the castle grounds unless invited. But all that would change after the pool party, when stores and commercial trading would take place with the proposed development plans including aquatic, health centres and medieval shops. Bit by bit, Alfred was looking at building a residual income he could retire on.

The last day at home, Alfred finished the markings on the lawn turf. The young Germans had settled in, Margareta was happy. Happy wife, happy life, and Alfred was back to work knowing what he did best for the moment.

THE FLIGHT

Saying his farewells to Margareta and giving the job list to the young Germans with *"auf weidersehen,"* goodbye in German, Alfred loaded his three heavy bags into the shuttle, got in, closed the door, and pointed the driver in the direction of the Rockhampton airport. A second trip in two days, one being for Ikav and now himself.

What was in Alfred's bags was a mystery. Could there be rocks as the bags were slightly bulging? But Alfred wasn't or hadn't been doing rock sampling. However, it must have been important to take them to the site.

The shuttle van stopped. Alfred opened the door, the shuttle driver helped with Alfred's bags.

"My goodness, sir, what do you have in these bags?"

"Samples," was the only reply the driver heard from Alfred, whatever that meant.

Alfred made his way to the check in for the mining charterflight that morning. With a trolley and a bit of a push, he managed to get them to the check in desk. Placing the bags on the scales, they weighed in at over one hundred kilograms, and a hasty reply came back from the staff at the service desk.

"Sir, you realise these bags exceed your allocated weight, well over sixty kilograms."

Alfred replied sturdily, "These bags contain items the company has asked me to bring as necessary freight ordered and if you wish to debate this with the company, go right ahead. The refusal of allowing this extra weight will only jeopardise your future contract with them."

Alfred had them by the short and curlies. He knew they would scan his bags and contents, as they were priority of course, but everything inside would all be legitimate.

Taken a little aback, the check in staff replied, "Certainly, Mr. Norris, we apologise for a misunderstanding. No need to bother management. We will get your bags to the mine. Is there anything else we can do for you, Mr. Norris?"

"As a matter of fact, there is," replied Alfred. "The business lounge, I would like to relax a little before the flight with two colleagues. We are company representatives on this flight, and this would make a lasting impression on your performance."

"Certainly, Mr. Norris."

With a satisfied smile, Alfred turned and walked away with Ernie and Drew. And this is how Alfred was able to negotiate his excess luggage on the mining charter.

We still didn't know what was inside those bags apart from personal jocks and socks with company uniforms.

However, Alfred with his man bag and his two work colleagues entered the business lounge and would discuss a number of topics as they relaxed. This time, work issues and prospective job interviews. Two positions had opened for top performing tradesmen in the electrical and technical fields on site.

You may ask what this had to do with Alfred and his colleagues. Well, Alfred and his two colleagues were on the selection committee. Of course, that was what was in the bag, the interview papers we suspect were in the weighted bag with other things.

As Alfred and his colleagues Ernie and Drew went through the security scanners, this time round Alfred had forgotten to tell security he had steel pins in the bones of his lower leg. It had been from a horse riding accident, all those years ago on a wild brumby, the one that had caused Alfred to disappear for a few days. Alfred had usually declared his steel parts as he called himself the "man of steel," but this time, he must have forgotten as he had been talking to Ernie and Drew. The alarm bells started flashing. Immediately Alfred knew what happened and advised security there were no metal items in his pocket only in his body.

The security team on this swing were not the usual team he dealt with and they thought Alfred was carrying some sophisticated weapon in his body. Taking the matter seriously before Alfred had a chance to explain, the security were nearly going to take him aside to strip search him when Ernie called out.

"Wait a minute, Alfred has steel pins in his legs from a riding accident."

How could Ernie ever forget? Alfred reminded him every time he saw him at the airport.

This was immediately confirmed and another close call for Alfred.

Alfred had trained for every iron man competition in recent years. He might not have been the fastest competitor running and swimming with lumps of steel inside him, but he sure gave his competitors a run for their money.

Having said that, a complimentary pass in the business lounge at Rockhampton airport was more than enough for Alfred to consolidate his thoughts for the week ahead and the activities. A brief period of rain had been forecasted. Talking with Ernie and Drew about the activities down in the coal pit, around the coal pit, workshop rebuilds, with the possibility of inclement weather, Alfred completely got lost in thought and forgot his man bag was sitting under the chair next to him.

With an early lunch, an ice coffee in hand, downed by a lemon lime and bitters which Ernie and Drew finished on as well, a boarding call was called, but Alfred kept singing.

I love to have a rum with Ernie
I love to have a rum with Ernie
we slosh in moderation
and we never ever get roll in over
we drink in the town and business lounge
where the atmosphere is great
I love to have a rum with Ernie
cause Ernie's me mate yes.

I love to have a rum with Drew
I love to have a rum with Drew
we slosh in moderation
and we never ever get roll in over
we drink in the town and business lounge
where the atmosphere is great
I love to have a rum with Drew
because Drew is me mate, yes.

"Customers travelling on Skytrain to Nandi mine, boarding is commencing at gate 5. Please have your boarding passes ready."

The three men including Alfred were quickened to remove themselves from the lounge, thanking the staff from the business lounge desk and speeding toward the gate. In his rush, Alfred forgot something really important, his man bag. Fortunately, someone picked his bag up and had handed it to the staff at the lounge check in counter.

"Mr Alan Chuck Norris, can you please report to the service desk at the sky train business lounge?"

Realising his bag had mistakenly been left at the business lounge, Alfred turned back and ran back towards the business lounge. As he entered, the lady with the friendly smile called out, "I believe this is your bag, Mr. Norris."

With a pleasant smile and a thank you, Alfred ran back through the lounge doors towards the departing gate. The passengers had been boarding, and then then the call came, "Would a Mr. Alfred Norris please report to staff at gate 5? Gate closing in five minutes."

That was the shortest boarding call Alfred had even heard. Alfred ran, avoiding ladies with prams, little kids, and elderly ladies, apologising as he ran. Alfred had to make that flight.

Alfred sprinted, nearly knocking an old lady down in his persistent pacing towards the departure gate. An extreme apology was given as Alfred turned around, nearly running into a cleaner at the same time.

"Come on, Mr. Norris, you are the last to board," called the flight attendant once again. "The gate is just about to close."

Leading Alfred down a spiral set of stairs and onto the tarmac where the Dash 8 was about to start up its gas turbine engines, Alfred was quickly led up the stairwell and inside the cabin. As he entered, Alfred's work colleagues cheered as he walked down the aisle to his seat number 8A.

"Alfred, why is it you are always the last person on board?" called a work colleague.

"Probably because I'm the most important person on board and they need to wait for me," Alfred replied.

Then everybody laughed.

Alfred had made it.

Then the safety brief came after the door had closed on the Dash 8. Just before then, Alfred decided to push the call button. A cup of water was necessary as Alfred was dehydrating fast from all his rushing around. Seeing an emergency had nearly arisen, the emergency was fast tracked to give Alfred and Drew a bottle of water by each cabin crew member.

Now, for a brief moment, Alfred would close his eyes with head back on the seat, thinking of what he had forgotten from home, if anything, before the announcement would come across the PA system by cabin crew for preparing the aircraft for landing into the mining airport.

But just as the safety brief had been called for departure, the safety brief for descending into the mining airport came just as quickly. An hour had gone by. It seemed only a blink of an eye when Alfred heard the descent brief.

"Well, Drew," said Alfred. "Another tour of duty for seven days."

Drew just nodded his head.

As the Dash 8 was on final approach, something out of the ordinary happened. It had been raining, and the pilots had noticed some objects that had been floating across the runway. It had been reported that the greenies had been ramping up their protesting in the last few days. Could they have sabotaged the runway with dangerous objects? Within three hundred feet, the captain decided to abort the landing to make a go around. He had immediately contacted the mines Airport Runway Officer on the HF radio and had reported strange objects to be cleared before he could land.

Alfred had glanced on the off chance out the window and was staggered at what he saw, toilet rolls floating across the runway, as the pilot aborted the landing to make a go around.

"Trevor," Alfred called out to the seat in front of him. "We didn't get rid of those toilet rolls after the Flying Doctors came and went that night. They are floating across the runway."

The work colleagues thought it was hilarious, but the crew didn't seem to think so. An aborted landing meant a lot of dollars at the airline company's expense in a go around, even if it was for safety reasons.

Alfred not only had a please explain when on the ground, but an urgent call had also come through on Alfred's mobile from Margareta. The message had come through the Telstra reception in the air even with Alfred's phone on flight mode.

Alfred knew a complaint would be made to the maintenance superintendent from the airline and he had to think up something fast. The airline did not know why the toilet rolls had been there in the first place and this did give Alfred some cover. Also the problem with Margareta would have to be juggled into the equation as well. Emergencies at home were a priority.

The Dash 8 did land safely and taxied up to the mining airport office.

Alfred's colleagues were still laughing as they disembarked and walked across the tarmac.

"Alfred, there may be a shortage so go easy on those toilet rolls," one of his colleagues called out.

Fortunately, the aircrew didn't click on. "We hope you enjoyed the flight. Have a great week. We will see you in a week's time."

The bus was waiting, Alfred was hurrying to get reception so he could ring Margareta and tell her he has arrived safely, then he would ask through her translator what the problem was. This seemed like a plan. In Alfred's mind, Margareta made a big issue out of small things.

The protesters had camped near the airport and were ready to take on the mining company, but the heavens had opened and a swamping of their campsite with sleeping bags floating down the river that day and more consistent rain on the way was making any protest difficult.

For Alfred, the week was going to be full of opportunities, he reflected as he sat with his eyes closed for that ten-minute drive back to camp. Then he remembered Margareta.

Alfred quickly rang Margareta and as usual, her interpreter answered the phone.

"Why the urgent phone call, Margareta?" called Alfred.

"He's gone," yelled Margareta, through the interpreter.

"Who?" replied Alfred.

"The gardener," yelled Margareta through the interpreter.

For a moment, Alfred thought he was one of the young German tourists come to work on the castle estate.

"He's pinched all the spinach, thinking it was marijuana, and bolted."

Spinach would be a bit rough to smoke, thought Alfred, *and he must be a bit desperate for a joint, or maybe he was a bit confused*. At least there were still four of them left to help Margareta and her interpreter.

"Don't panic, Margareta, we can grow some more spinach," replied Alfred. "At least he hasn't been caught rolling it and smoking in around the castle."

A point to note was, the young German had neglected to put into practice Alfred's gardening tips. There was a small plantation and Alfred had given clear instructions on how to maintain it. Alfred had also wanted a garden for his lovely Margareta, but from all the hours of hard work from the market gardening side of the castle, this young German had taken it upon himself to remove property that he was entrusted to look after in good faith. It had been pointed out to all the young German tourists before they were given contracts to sign, that what's in the castle stays in the castle grounds. If there was a breach of contract, Alfred and Margareta had no choice but to dismiss the employee effective immediately. No redundancy and no compensation and they had agreed.

Wir stimmen ihren allgemeinen geschäftsbedingungen zu.

In other words, we agree to your terms and conditions.

One Gerry messed it up for the rest.

Now background security checks would be necessary for anyone coming to work on the premises.

However, the young German did leave a note out of courtesy.

Auf wiedersehen, danke für die arbiet.

Goodbye, thanks for the work.

But there was no forwarding address.

It wasn't going from one crisis to the next in Alfred's mind, it was sorting out priorities.

Alfred had on his mind now finalising the pool party for the castle, the bobsled sponsorship and trading in as much crypto currency as possible, not forgetting the horses. The workload with refuelling cart, generators, and vehicle rebuilds in the workshop fitted somewhere in the middle.

Achieving goals was Alfred's prime objectives on this week and if anyone didn't meet those expectations, there would be an Alfred wake up slap. Yes, a slap in the right direction by Alfred.

It had been raining heavily across the site and extra safety precautions were needed. The workshop was muddy and the machinery slippery from a continued pounding of rain.

This was a good time for Alfred and yes, Ikav was back on the scene to consolidate the paperwork.

The paperwork meant fuel calculations. The parts list meant vehicles to service. The weather though was a problem.

The first meeting came that morning. Alfred, Ikav, Drew and Ernie were all over it with safety.

"Slip, slop and slap" was the safety theme, meaning sunscreen on a sunny day.

Alfred's theme: "Don't slip, don't be sloppy and if anyone is sloppy, give them a slap"

This went down as the safety focus after all the work details were assigned, and the sign on sheets were all done.

Alfred then added his bit in about focus on work, team effort and the pool party was the following week. There was an extra charter flight going to Rocky for those who had registered for the party and of course the ride on mower race. If there was anyone who had registered but couldn't make it at the last minute, to advise Alfred's catering staff immediately with a contact number listed below as they needed to know for catering purposes.

This was a private miners' pool party, not a secret policeman's ball.

But work now for the next seven days of mining contracts were the priority, and so Alfred and his colleagues would start working shift down the pit, in the workshops, on the breakdown pads with the heavy machinery with this song:

Now Alfred is a wanderer
and it's in a miner's blood too
and that's why Alfred goes driving along as happily
as long as he can do.

Happy days, happy days.
Ah happy, happy, happy
happy days, happy days.
Alfred loved those team happy days.

Now fuelling trucks and fixing carts creates a fresh
desire as Alfred has a healthy heart.
His chest breathes freely outside.

His big wide mouth sings happily as he motors
along the haul road.

Happy days, happy days, happy days.
Ah happy happy happy happy days.
Alfred loved those team happy days.

Now Alfred's mouth sings happily.
Why is a little bird singing to you?
Such a joyful song.
Such a pleasant song through the countryside
which it moves.

Be on your way, be on your way.
Be on your way little bird
or I'll have you for dinner now.

And that was Alfred's happy day.

You might have noticed now Alfred was becoming quite a confident singer. Even Trevor, Drew and Ernie passed on some positive take fives and not hazard cards any more about Alfred's singing. It was a morale booster for all the team. Even Alfred couldn't believe what he was singing, let alone his repertoire of songs he was focusing on.

The day came when Alfred and Ikav were involved in a hit and run accident on site.

No, it wasn't the protesters from their hippy huts and smoking camps, but two half-asleep kangaroos on the mining road in the dark. Startled, they ran off and then jumped right back into Alfred and Ikav's refuelling cart. With quick reactions, Alfred didn't take his eyes off the road and kept motoring on. One kangaroo got away, possibly with a sore head; the other became the mascot imbedded in the truck bull bar. It was more like one kangaroo got hit and remained inside the bull bar frame and the other one ran.

Having refuelled the Gensets around the site and a few vehicles, driving back to the workshop with a kangaroo hanging off the bull bar, an environmental and wildlife report would have to be made with the key eye witnesses. Of course this would be Ikav.

Alfred thought, *Fortunately this isn't a female kangaroo with a Joey in the pouch. But a Joey! Why do they call a baby kangaroo in the pouch a Joey and not a Freddy, or a Teddy, or a Gerry?*

This has to do with the first sightings of kangaroos on this continent. A man called Joey took a shine to a baby kangaroo where the mother was shot or badly injured. He looked after the baby kangaroo and passed his name on to the baby kangaroo to become a Joey. This was Alfred's reasoning.

Just think, who would follow after Alfred? Could he leave his mark on history not in a pouch but from his castle? Only time would tell, if he didn't have any more problems with the council and environmentalists.

Ikav was thinking more along the lines of kangaroo sausages with fresh roadkill. He could be stripping the carcass in between breaks. This would have to be done after Alfred made the incident report.

It's great to have a ring of friends that have got your back, thought Alfred. You could call it the ring of confidence. With friends like this, you could sleep well at night and not have to look over shoulder during the day on who's going to find faults with you.

Life is great, Alfred thought.

Till someone came annoying him, and that happened to be a supervisor from the other crew who was about to fly home.

"We need more detail on the kangaroo incident, Alfred," said the supervisor who we won't name.

Some people have just got to make a name for themselves as this was so in Alfred's eyes.

Alfred's own supervisor was a lovely fellow who cared about his crew and Alfred himself had great respect for him as did all his other work colleagues, the kangaroo incident was the least of his own supervisor's concerns. So just to make a point of what more detail Alfred could give, Alfred thought, *Is this guy for real? How far is this supervisor willing to go?*

Then it dawned on Alfred, *I can make a story out of this. This supervisor made such a song and dance about the kangaroo, I can give it to him ending in a song.*

Watch the kangaroos feed, Jack.
Watch the kangaroos feed.
There a dangerous breed, Jack.
Watch the kangaroos feed.

All together now.
Tie the kangaroo down, Jack.
Tie the kangaroo down.
Tie the kangaroo down, Jack.
Tie the kangaroo down.

Would this be enough for the final part of the written report? Alfred thought. The kangaroo was tied down on the frame of the bull bar as they were feeding alongside the road.

The next day a meeting had been called by the union delegate onsite. Had there been any specific items of concern for the fitters, boiler makers, electricians, fuel cart operators? he had asked.

The electricians had been called with service cart operators for an incident that was a concern to safety.

Ricardo the electrician spoke up. "We need more power, Alfred, we need more power."

It began to seem like Scotty off *Star Trek* talking to Captain James Kirk.

The next minute he will be saying, "Beam me up, Alfred."

What Ricardo was really trying to say: "We need more generators for lighting and communications towers. There needs to be more lighting for safety in and around the pit."

Then came the grievances for the wet conditions and how the company was going to compensate them if they couldn't get home.

A genius idea came to Alfred. It was as though a light had flashed on. "We need to pool the talent. We could have a talent quest or show in the wet mess at the camp to keep morale up, when wet conditions persist."

There came a few grumbles and a few laughs. Then someone came up with this: "This would provide a safety mechanism for the theme 'look after your mates.' Make sure they are okay."

Great idea, Alfred. This would be better than Trivial Pursuit. This was noted in the safety minutes.

Next on the union safety agenda. Night shift had been losing sleep because of activities during the day around the camp. There were some pretty heavy moving people who walked like elephants, talked as if they were yelling and slammed the doors every time they left their room and entered their room.

Alfred came up with an idea, after talking with his colleagues.

"When these people have had a few beers, give them a sleeping pill and a laxative on the same night and ensure they compensate for any damage done to the bed and bedding in the morning. If there is any trouble, security will be on hand."

Somehow this may fix the problem of sleep deprivation for the rest of the night shift workers. As for traffic and cleaners, they would be told in no uncertain terms to keep the noise to a minimum, as sleep is a safety necessity for night shift workers and any deprivation of sleep could cause safety issues on site.

By the time the union delegate had got to the bottom of all the concerns, a deal was settled with management. This of course would be a win win once again for all.

This time round, Alfred's contribution to the safety meeting had also come from consulting all his colleagues, Trevor Keen, Ikav, Ernie and Drew. Not to mention a few other compatriots.

And happy wife, happy life. Alfred had not been interrupted by any phone calls from Margareta in the last five hours. Things could change quite dramatically with Margareta's fiery temper.

Margareta didn't understand the significance of the saying, "When in Rome, do what the Romans do." In Australia, do what the Australians do. Not in Australia, do what the Spanish do. Alfred had been breaking her in gradually. Alfred had also visiting hours and days for Margareta at the castle and shopping hours so she could get about with her interpreter. In time, she would talk Aussie, not to be associated with an English accent, as Margareta never got over what the English did to her great-great-great-grandfather's Spanish galleon ship when he was holidaying with his family in South America all those centuries ago. The problem is that the Spanish always seem to want their gold and artefacts stolen from them by the English, but they, the Spanish, never seem to consider the fact that they stole and pillaged first from South American indigenous people.

Harbouring grudges always backfires, so Margareta was slowly being coached by Alfred to learn about history. Spain's reputation in this time was not admirable.

Back to site, Alfred had his reputation to live up to as well. His consultation with management and colleagues were free as his expertise was nowhere to be matched.

Alfred was gradually getting his office facilities as with the electricians on site. A computer, a laptop for field work, a company phone as required. This was part of Alfred's new employment package as he was taking on more responsibilities.

Writing up a program for fuel cart procedures and what to do when there is an environmental spill, the manhandling, what precautions were needed to be taken in wet weather, and how to abate misinformation when it came to manhandling, precautions needed to be taken, especially when wildlife was involved. Also taking into account snake activity at certain times of the year. A snake kit must be carried alongside the first aid kit. Why?

Because Alfred nearly had had a medical misadventure once when one of his colleagues was bit by a snake.

THE SNAKE ATTACK

One night shift, a colleague was relieving himself. Talk about being in the wrong place at the wrong time. He was watering the area where two snakes were mating and unwittingly got bitten on the family jewels in the dark. He looked down at the sharp pain with a torch; there were two puncture marks. The snakes were seen moving away. A screeching call could be heard meters away by Alfred.

"Help, Alfred, help."

In a panic, not thinking about his own safety, Alfred came running.

"What's wrong, Kelvin?"

"Take a look down there, I've been bitten by a snake."

Not a pretty sight, thought Alfred.

"Did you see what sort of snake it was, Kelvin?" asked Alfred.

"It wasn't a one-eyed trouser snake, it was a brown snake," said Kelvin in his delirious state. "You got to get help, Alfred."

"Don't panic, Kelvin," called Alfred, "place this bandage around your you-know-what, leave the bite exposed and sit down. I'll call for the paramedics on the radio."

Alfred called an emergency on site. The radios went silent for the state of emergency.

"Emergency, emergency, emergency," called Alfred.

"What is your name and nature of the emergency?" came the reply on the emergency channel.

"My name is Alfred Chuck Norris, man down with snake bite. We are on the southern side roading of the pit near dispatch, need urgent medical assistance," called Alfred calmly.

In response, a paramedic came on the emergency channel.

"Alfred, is it. I want you to stay calm and do everything I tell you to do before we can get there, okay," called the paramedic. "Firstly, collect any venom from around the wound so we can identify what snake for the anti-venom. Secondly, the unconventional way is to suck the venom out or he will die."

Now there was a long pause. This was going from bad to worse. Kelvin was going to die.

Alfred dropped the radio and ran to Kelvin.

"Alfred, are you there?" called the paramedic "Come in, Alfred."

Now the paramedics were starting to panic.

The sirens were flashing, the emergency vehicle was racing to the other side of the pit. All heavy equipment was standing down for the emergency and here was poor Alfred with the balance of life in his hand.

Running towards Kelvin, Alfred thought Kelvin was going to die.

"What did they say, Alfred, what did they say?" called Kelvin in pain.

Alfred called out, "You're going to die, Kelvin."

"What else did he say, Alfred?"

"I got to suck the poison out or you'll die."

"That's better," screamed Kelvin. "You got to suck it out."

Just as Alfred was about to suck the venom out with his eyes closed, the paramedics turned up just in time.

"Good job, Alfred, we'll take it from here," called the paramedic.

They had then identified the snake venom as from a brown snake. Very serious and in the wrong spot of the abdomen.

A relieved Alfred and a nearly sick Alfred returned to the fuel truck. Did Alfred need counselling, yes?

The paramedics were able to neutralise the snake bite, but they needed to get Kelvin to hospital urgently. The Royal Flying Doctors were called in once again. They would be there in the hour, flying through the night. They would find a well-lit runway this time at the Nandi mine site and not flamed toilet rolls.

Kelvin was flown out that night to Townsville base hospital by the Royal Flying Doctors. Kelvin also survived the bite with one ball less and a higher pitched voice.

But if it wasn't for Alfred's quick thinking that night, the situation could have been a little different, a fatality that would have been on Alfred's conscience. What would he have told poor Kelvin's wife? That he had second thoughts about removing venom from a snake bite?

When Alfred had got back to the workshop that night, he had to be isolated from the rest of the crew for counselling, as they couldn't contain themselves from laughing. They couldn't show initially as Alfred was in a state of shock however he did get through it and was a better man for it.

There was a paper trail as the incident had to be reported, recorded. Fortunately a pictorial picture was not necessary only an explanation of the events and they would be kept as brief as possible.

Did Alfred learn something from this? Yes. A snake kit should be carried at all times in a vehicle. Don't venture out in the dark with no lighting. There is wild life all around. If it wasn't a snake, it could have been a dingo looking for dinner.

Alfred did eventually win an award for this safety interaction and Kelvin would return to site, recovered and with a slightly different tone of voice.

The next three days would keep Alfred and Ikav busy around the pit and in the workshop. Alfred's prototype bobsled was almost complete as well. This had now been under way over the last six months on nights only. Those in between hours under strict company security in a small lockable contained workshop, would give Alfred and team now made up of six, the ability to create a bobsled never seen before. This would take shape with new aerodynamics with a copyright to follow.

We cannot show you the complete picture as it is under

copyright. But we can show the initial stages.

Alfred was also keeping the team's training together under secrecy: the gym workouts, the lap training at the camp which he
was timing for every individual. The timed run around the camp
was improving each night on day shift and mornings on night
shift, with the odd collision of an unsuspecting person walking
out in front of the team. Each team member had a code name.
Out of the six there was Tarzan, Benson, Boris, Jerico, Jasper,
Finley, and Nimrod. Only they would answer to their names.
These were fitters, tyre fitters, electricians, and an office worker.
Alfred's motto is "Variety is the spice of life" and he would train
them hard. Even on their breaks, he had a regular fitness routine
for the six to keep in shape. And to keep in shape they did, as
they would be wearing the company logo to qualify for the Winter Olympics in Japan.

Where did Alfred get his determination, vision, passion from?

Keep reading as you will find out. Alfred comes from a long
line of achievers. His grandfather was an arm-wrestling champion; his father, a trapeze artist; and his mother, a fashion designer
who won a number of awards. His brother Hector is an artist who
specialises in fabric colours, so you can see Alfred has no shortages of ideas when it comes to putting a team together.

His Grandfather the strong man, his father the bouncer, his
mother makes the team uniforms and his brother paints the team
and company logos.

Watch this space. Things are going to get interesting as to
finding out whether they can find a training venue on the ice in
sunny Queensland or maybe the team will have to travel inter-
state to find the ice.

Alfred's code name: ICEMAN.

THE RUNAWAY HAUL TRUCK

This swing for Alfred and his colleagues, it seemed like there was no shortage of incidents.

The fourth night, a haul truck had just been refuelled by a service cart up on one of the service pads. Alfred and Ikav following in a service truck within a fifty-meter spacing when the three-hundred-ton haul truck pulled out from the service pad. Call sign T 05.

For some reason, the dump truck had pulled over to the left and Ikav called up, "Truck 05 light vehicle coming round on your left."

There was no response. The dump truck was stationary till Alfred had passed it. Then, for some reason, as Alfred had passed in the refuelling cart, it began to move in behind them.

Alfred and Ikav were moving from generator to generator round the pit and the Cat 976 haul truck kept following. There was no radio call from T 05 and dispatch was trying to get hold of the driver.

Alfred and Ikav T05 were called up by dispatch and realised they had passed T05 just off the refuelling pad. Was this T 05 behind them? Alfred called dispatch, advising T05 was behind them in the fuel truck 27 and would try and make contact.

"Truck 05, you got a copy," called Alfred.

No reply.

Alfred called up again. "Truck 05, you got a copy."

Alfred's fuel cart was still being followed by what he thought was Truck 05.

"Dispatch, fuel cart 27 here, Truck 05 is behind us, and has been behind us for the last ten minutes. We'll drive up on a dump pad where it's flat, circle and get up alongside him or her. Who's driving Truck 05 Dispatch?"

"The driver's name is Harry Potter."

There was silence for a minute whilst Alfred and Ikav collected their thoughts on that name.

"Dispatch, there is no wizardry involved in that name, is there?"

There was silence then for a minute.

"No, he is one of the new drivers," came the voice from dispatch.

"I don't know if they picked up what was said about Harry Potter, but next they will be telling us that we are involved in Lord of the Rings," said Alfred to Ikav who just sat back laughing. "And we are involved in the sequel," said Alfred.

"Harry, truck 05, you got a copy," as Alfred called again.

No reply.

"Dispatch, we may have an emergency here," called Alfred. "We are approaching a flat area on the dump pad, so we will circle and when he follows, we will drive alongside him and see if we can get Harry's attention."

"We will send in emergency services," called dispatch.

Now Alfred had this idea. It was a crazy idea, but if they couldn't stop the truck, someone would need to climb the emergency ladder to get inside and stop the moving truck and find out what the problem is with the driver.

Now Alfred didn't want to be called a hero as this was just an idea. Ikav would take the wheel and Alfred would get alongside the emergency ladder as Ikav held the fuel truck steady.

"Are you crazy, Alfred? You're not James Bond, Alfred," called Ikav.

"And neither are you, Ikav," replied Alfred. "It's now or never."

Alfred nearly broke out singing Elvis's song, "It's now or never..."

"We are on the pad now," Alfred radioed dispatch. "And we are going to drive up alongside truck 05."

"Copy that," replied dispatch. "Emergency vehicle and paramedic are on their way, Fuel Cart 27."

Alfred acknowledged and got Ikav to take the wheel as Alfred got into a position alongside Truck 05 to jump and mount the emergency ladder. There was no other way of stopping the truck before something drastic happened.

"Alfred, you sure you are going to be okay?" called Ikav.

"Sure, just a little closer, Ikav," called Alfred. "I'm going to jump now."

And so Alfred made the daring jump straight into the emergency ladder.

Ikav pulled slightly away whilst Alfred climbed the ladder.

The haul truck 05 was going round and round in circles on the pad as Alfred reached the top of the ladder and was heading for the driver's side of the cab.

The area had been cleared by dispatch as emergency vehicles would arrive and that area of the pad around haul truck 05 would be cordoned off for safety investigation.

To Alfred's surprise, the driver Harry Potter was still staring out the front of the cab with a smile on his face. He hadn't noticed him walking toward the cab until Alfred opened the cab door and Harry nearly fell out sideways.

This is weird, Alfred thought. Then Alfred realised Harry had had a stroke. Quickly realising this, Alfred took charge and pushed Harry to one side, managed to get over him, applied the electric breaking till haul truck 05 came to a stop, then switched off the ignition, applying the park brake.

Alfred's adrenalin was pumping and Harry still had a smile on his face.

Ikav pulled up alongside the haul truck, placed the hazard lights on and called, "Nice job, Alfred, nice job. Another safety report to write out, Alfred. That's two in two nights," called Ikav.

"You're a witness too," called Alfred.

"I'll drop the electric ladder," Alfred called, "and will carry Harry down the stairwell."

"I'm coming," called Ikav.

Harry still had a pulse, his eyes were blinking, hands still locked out in front of him as though he was driving, a smile on his face. Fortunately he wasn't a big man, maybe a man in his mid-thirties but somehow had had a stroke after refuelling and was trying to signal he needed help.

Ikav was big and strong enough to carry Harry over his shoulders.

Just as Ikav and Alfred were coming down the stairwell with Harry, the emergency vehicles and paramedics pulled up.

The paramedic called out to Alfred, "Alfred, twice in two nights you're on the scene!" as they carried Harry on the stretcher into the paramedics' four-wheel land cruiser, still with a smile on his face and arms out in front of him.

"We will take it from here," called the paramedic.

"Harry, can you hear me?" yelled the paramedic.

"He can't but I certainly can," replied Alfred.

The mine emergency had been called, the flying doctors had been called again and now Alfred and Ikav had to give a statement once more, whilst operators and maintenance were being briefed in the crib hut.

The operator superintendent was addressing the operators in the crib hut on the situation at hand. Their colleague Harry Potter had been the driver at hand. The operators couldn't get over their colleague's name Harry Potter, thinking there was some wizardry involved. This was the third emergency called in the last three months and the latest two were on this night shift.

There was no wizardry, only Alfred and this time Ikav on the scene of the incident. Matter of fact, Alfred had had something to do with every incident follow up. Could Alfred be the Wizard?

A cat 796 haul truck has blind spots. The driver cannot see any-one coming up from the right, in front and below and behind, al-though he has a reverse camera only. Light vehicles keep a fifty-meter distance behind.

The final safety review of all the incidents would come out in Alfred's report. Alfred would also give his interpretations on how safety would be better achieved in the future.

Some more pearls of wisdom coming from Alfred once again. The company could not afford to lose Alfred now as well as Ikav. New contracts were drawn up for Alfred and Ikav plus a bonus on performance when Alfred gave of his best to maintain utmost safety for everyone, although Alfred was still coming to grips with the snake incident.

But for Alfred this was getting to be beyond a joke, as he was committed to the bobsled project which was his retirement plan, and of course finalising the pool party activities and participation of competitors, not to mention the miners and guests coming. This would take place as soon as he arrived home in a few days.

Now you might think Alfred was getting a bit overcautious of any other event happening before he went home Wednesday morning, but this wasn't so. Alfred contemplated now his every move on site. He was given his job description at every pass meeting and he could work this with his eyes blindfolded, except driving around the site of course.

There was also someone studying and taking notes on Alfred, how he handled every situation, his approach to his work colleagues and his ability to create. Maybe it was the supervisor, or maybe someone under cover, time would tell.

THE PROJECTS

There was a new fuel project coming. The fuel handlers and re-fuelers would be called in as part of the effort to summarise the best ideas. It was called the Fuel Farm Projects. More infrastructure and heavy mining equipment meant more fuel farms on site.

Alfred had another idea. Out of the three fuel farms, they reserved two fuel carts for each fuel farm, that way they could keep the fuel farms balanced in their tank body consumption. Road trains could balance the volume of fuel up between the three fuel farms quite quickly.

Alfred, you've done it again. You're not the fuel tank, you're the think tank. Not only are you saving the company money, your bobsled investment is paying off.

The last four nights had taken a toll on Alfred. He was beginning to show signs of weariness. Ikav, Trevor, Drew and Ernie had begun to see this in Alfred as they knew he had only a few days to finalise the events for the pool party at the castle. This was a significant event for D crew and invited guests. Alfred could not stop now. They needed to cover for Alfred, and cover they did.

Alfred was also given a mental fatigue test by the paramedics and he had only just passed it with a few bad jokes. But he did get through it question by question.

Back at the workshop that night, Ikav, Trevor, Drew, and Ernie had decided to quietly make a cardboard replica of Alfred, so that there could be seen some sort of resemblance of him in the dark sitting in the passenger's seat smiling. To most people driving past the fuel cart, it seemed as though Alfred had a frozen smile on his face and never moved his head.

When the fuel cart came back to the workshop for Alfred and

Ikav to do some repair work, Drew and Ernie would wake Alfred up from Alfred's convenient resting area, wherever that might be, to bring him back into action. No one else knew Alfred was punching out a few "Zs" and the team kept it that way for the remaining two nights.

Alfred and the team had managed to get through the night. Ikav had helped to get Alfred his well-deserved hours of sleep in his hideaway before getting him back to camp for the day's sleep. The company was always emphasising fatigue management, Alfred had taken full advantage of this and still lived up to his reputation, just with a little help from his friends. Yes, Alfred had managed to get half a night's sleep as well as getting the day's sleep after night shift.

Maybe that cardboard replica of Alfred needed to stay on site a bit longer.

Alfred and his colleagues, under their very grateful supervisor, did finish the last two nights successfully without any more emergencies. The maintenance team had survived another tour of duty without casualties, that was a plus. Then it began to rain.

Alfred had two flashbacks involving the boat he had built in the workshop all those years ago and his swimming pool. It was about to be filled with water from the heavens. The boat had floated and Alfred had been advised the plumbing work had been completed, the power had been certified.

One last concern, the moat. The moat was designed to discharge any heavy rain or flooding, but he hadn't given much thought about the crocodiles in it when it came to flooding discharge. Alfred only hoped that the crocodiles would float out with the storm water or the neighbours would get a little upset. Not many of them had pet crocodiles around the house.

Oh well, Alfred thought. That was the worst-case scenario, maybe he was thinking the worst.

They were all flying out in the morning. Or were they not as the rain got heavier?

THE POOL PARTY

The flight was delayed by a few hours back to Rockhampton that Wednesday morning, but by the afternoon, with a few extra charter flights to clear the backlog of stranded miners and the weather clearing, all flights to Townsville and Rockhampton were made.

Alfred made it home. Ikav, Drew, Ernie and Trevor Keen also made it back to Townsville and Cairns. A well-deserved break.

After being picked up at Rockhampton airport by his arranged taxi driver, the road home was all Alfred wanted to see. Alfred would break the news of events over the last week to Margareta gently as she would have had full catering services, orchestral quartets, a trumpeter to open the racing events, not the horse racing but the ride on mower events and the decorations, to attend to.

The German tourists had settled in with the Bavarian look, the dress style, the men on shorts, braces with long socks and feathered hat for the occasion and the two women in long white dress with short sleeves and blouses with enough cleavage to turn any man on. Margareta would keep it very seemly as this was the dress for the occasion, not for working around the castle grounds.

Margareta knew what miners were like and asked Alfred to keep any rush of excitement down and to stay focused on the pool celebrations and the ride on mower race. The rest would follow suite.

So there we have it, Alfred is staging for a pool party showdown in three days' time.

The lighting effects had been discussed with the Civil Aviation Safety Authority. There would be no high beam lights that would shine into the faces of any oncoming aircraft on the approach to Rockhampton airport.

The lit-up pool area would be the new Civil Aviation Safety Authority way point for any aircraft established on the approach for Rockhampton airport, with of course the cheery red danger light on top of the castle indicating castle height above sea level and obstruction point again to any aircraft on the approach. This was a win win for all. A milestone completed for Alfred. Alfred had even invited the office staff from the Australian Civil Aviation Safety Authority to the pool party. Unfortunately the offer had been declined due to commitments involved in Canberra, but a big thank you came from the staff, wishing Alfred well for the future. Alfred had also taken the initiative of having a prestigious photo of the castle, with pool lay out and castle racing grounds for anyone who had helped in the castle process and couldn't make the party. To his relief, ninety percent of the invitations had been accepted, and the castle photos were few. A cost savings for Alfred and Margareta.

The oldest of the guests were the stone masons. They would be honoured guests since they had laid the foundations.

The security for the night would be on their toes for infiltrators posing as guests, as a coded pass on each ticket could be veri-fied. The code itself was an encoded message different for each guest but registered on Margareta's data bank. Yes, Margareta was very professional in this area although she professed she didn't understand a word of English. I think we know better.

The last imposters trying to sneak across the drawbridge were council building inspectors. They got caught with cameras hidden inside the lining of their pockets. When confronted, they made some feeble excuses about recording some environment spill. The terminations were quick and effective. Going for a swim in the moat in the dark was not a good idea, especially with swim-ming lizards around.

That was the past, the present was before Alfred and his lovely Margareta who would entertain the guests, or should I say some of the guests would entertain the hosts with the ride on mower racing.

The lighting and features looked spectacular for the pool facilities. The pool itself was a lap swimming pool approximately forty meters long and two point five meters wide. It was specifically designed for Alfred's training program, not only for himself, to build up his arms and body strength but also for the bobsled team on weekend retreats. Oh yes, he had a training programme, a home away from home.

Back to the pool party venue. The orchestral sextet were preparing their Handel's water music with other background music for the pleasantries for the evening.

To make the evening a bit more fun, a fancy dress was part of the entry requirement. Miners were not to wear any mining gear as this was not seen as working hours.

This was now Friday night and the party was about to begin in the afternoon of Saturday.

Lines had been all marked out the day previous for the ride on mower race and the ride ons had all been transported to the castle. Before crossing the bridge, security had checked over the ride on mowers individually to ensure no foul play or hidden cameras.

Alfred was nowhere to be seen all that Friday. Could he have cold feet and not be attending his own party?

Alfred had disappeared into the bowels of the castle's undergirth. There had been a water blockage to the pool piping system, although in the last week there had been some considerable amounts of rain and the pool was only three quarters full. The water pump had stopped pumping water from the lower reservoir to the pool itself and Alfred, with one of his German tourists, had taken it upon himself to find out what the problem was.

As the moat had been flooded, there was something jammed between the meshing and the pump impeller. There was also a level screen that showed a visual presentation of anything floating or moving around the outer foundations and below the water level of the castle.

When Alfred and the German tourist Gert saw what was caus-ing the blockage, they started scratching their heads. Boris, who had left the castle unexpectedly with bags of spinach, thinking it was high grade marijuana, must have got that stoned, and he had fallen over the side of the drawbridge without anyone noticing. Even the crocodiles wouldn't touch him.

Boris, with eyes wide and a smile on his face, had got sucked into and along the side meshing and was blocking the water flow to be pumped. No wonder there had been no forwarding address.

Alfred was thinking this negative thought, which was against his principles: what else could go wrong before the pool party tomorrow. Maybe a few of the police force needed to be invited to keep an eye on any of the greenies, who in a state of drunken-ness, could fall into the moat on their protest campaign.

This had been Gert's friend. There was a sense of sadness, but he knew Boris would have gone out with a bang, a smile on his face, no matter what. This consoled Girt a little.

"Auf wiedersehen mein feund."

"Goodbye, my friend."

Family and friends would have to be notified prior to the ser-vice. For Boris, Germany had been a distant land now. He had lived with a sense of adventure, having travelled with his young German friends around the world and finally ending up in Queensland, Australia.

But the smoking of marijuana had taken Boris to the point of no return and to also losing his sense of smell, as this was so when he smoked a whole bag of spinach, thinking it was dried weed.

Boris would now have to be fished out from the moat side by police divers, as this now would be classed as a fatality. There would be no suspicious circumstances under investigation, only an accident incurred by Boris falling to his death whilst being stoned, as an autopsy would show.

The girls too would have been a little upset, although Boris knew the consequences of the marijuana plant. Boris had said it was always for a sickness he had acquired when he was a child, but never elaborated on what sickness. He said medical marijuana had been prescribed.

I don't think so, thought Alfred. *It was only prescribed so Boris could get high.*

Now with the blockage water problem found, the police were notified and their specialist divers would recover the body of Boris. A complete autopsy would be done on Boris and of course his relatives would be notified.

But Boris had been an orphan so Girt had said. His family were his friends and now they would have to say their goodbyes.

Alfred would have his pool filled just in time. By late Friday afternoon, the caterers had arrived; the light technicians would work the night installing a radiance of lights. Margareta and her staff had replanted the vegetable garden where Boris had uprooted the spinach and the flower arrangements for the weekend were in Bavarian style.

In Alfred's eyes, no stone had been unturned, the pool party being only twelve hours away.

The chief executive of Nandi mining and his staff would arrive by helicopter as promised, early that Saturday morning. The landing pad had a Red Cross on it just to confuse the greenies. The helicopter pad was on the second level of the castle.

As the official sponsors of the party, company delegates were required to make a presence and also to make the presentations later on in the evening. Then there would be the official opening of the pool of course.

The countdown was now on. Alfred and Margareta were expecting visitors to stay overnight as there were officially one hundred and twenty rooms, not to mention the downstairs dungeon for anyone who got a bit unruly.

The boxes were being ticked:
- Guest list invitations
- Flower arrangements

- Pool orchestra
- Seating arrangements
- Official podium
- The presentations
- The big dip (the final dip in the pool)
- The flashing lights
- The music and sound systems
- Car parking as arranged

The hydro power station would be pumping out a few kilowatts and the best thing about it, the neighbours wouldn't even know, as they were all attending the party. It was a good time to be had by all and Alfred was making some money on the hydro scheme.

The stone mason's plaque would be engraved on the entry to Alfred's castle, possibly for advertising. But as their age had caught up with the remaining three and Jimmy, who would be remembered as he had passed on, a mention of the ancient skills would also be highlighted at the presentations.

The awards would also be presented for the winner of the ride on mower race, the best costume, and the best actor.

The best actor? Watch this space.

Margareta had also gone to the trouble of asking the caterers about incorporating crocodile stew, and freshly harvested home grown meat from Alfred's moat. Also fresh local road kill, the meat of the day on the menu.

That Friday, Alfred didn't get much sleep. Then, there would be an early morning start on Saturday to ensure everything was in place.

There was only one way into Alfred's castle by road and that was across the drawbridge. The other way was by chopper, landing on the executives' pad.

There were a few passages out from the castle but those secrets were known by Alfred and the stone masons from the initial copies of the castle plans.

On a good note, all but one team member from D crew were coming. These were Alfred's work colleagues. Bert, the only team member that couldn't attend, had serious gout problems and was advised by his doctor to rest up. The medication prescribed didn't seem to do much. Alfred had this weird thought: *Maybe medical marijuana is beneficial after all. Who knows.*

Finally the morning came for the party activities. Alfred had a spring in his step. Margareta had made breakfast, Alfred's favourite, scrambled eggs, and baked beans. Everything was in order or so Alfred thought as he viewed the outer perimeters of the castle later from the observation platform. Alfred could see with his binoculars who would be approaching, entering, and exiting the castle grounds. The moment of truth awaited Alfred and Margareta. All his fundraising from investing his personal savings into his own personal crypto currencies, his horse racing techniques to bet on the right horses and now the power generation plant he had gone out of the way to build to remove customers such as his neighbours from a highly competitive power distribution market.

Yes, Alfred did have enemies: the banks that had closed their branches, the council building inspectors, and the greenies on the other side of the moat. *Who said life was easy?* Alfred thought. But Alfred did have one friend in the council on his side and that was the mayor. Ray Creswell had seen all the good things Alfred had done, as in cleaning up the environment, bringing a natural habitat to endangered species that needed to be fed consistently, creating a tourist attraction that would one day soon be open to the public and creating employment opportunities to young tourists who wanted to see a bit more of Australia. This meant bringing more revenue into the Rockhampton area with monies from off shore. So Ray Creswell would come to the informal function. We didn't know yet what his disguise would be but I'm sure he wouldn't be dressed up as the Lord Mayor ringing his bell as that would be a dead giveaway.

In and around Alfred's castle, it was preferred to have twelve-seater vans to bring a number of guests including D crew in, so there would be no problems with missing cars, floating cars in the moat, after a few Happy Hours.

Alfred wanted to keep the beverages to a few health drinks, as this would see his guests more stimulated for some fun than with too much alcohol consumption. No, it wasn't a cocktail to get high on either. It was pure vitamins as Alfred didn't want anyone in the pool drunk once it was opened, and he didn't want to pay out any compensation if someone drowned having been drunk.

Sensible idea, Alfred.

ON THE MENU

The food would be a variety from crock dishes, fish dishes including fish of the day, plant dishes, meat dishes (fresh roadkill). Steak would be cooked as per guest requirements, Alfred's policy being "Waste not, want not."

There would also be a salad bar, dessert area with fresh strawberries, ice cream, pavlovas, everything in the sweet arrangement. Margareta had gone to some trouble to incorporate some Spanish dishes. It would be a day for all.

The big screen was the next feature Alfred incorporated. Everything Alfred did was big and now the big screen, Alfred?

The event was being recorded live for any of the company staff that couldn't make it. Alfred not only thought about doing things big, he also had a big heart. The guests that couldn't make it would be able see the event live streamed.

THE SHOW DOWN

"Let the show begin," said Alfred. "The moment of truth."

By lunch time, a few of the guests who had travelled long and hard started to arrive.

The Townsville D crew team arrived, then came the Brisbane Sunshine Coast D crew team. The vans coming across the bridge were identified by the hire companies. Then came the Rocky D crew team. The home team, Alfred liked to call them. Lastly, the neighbours and associated guests.

There was a parking attendant on the castle side. Security had their outpost just off the road leading to the drawbridge with their sniffer dogs Bonnie and Clyde and a scanner. No one could get access across the drawbridge without going through Checkpoint Charlie.

No cameras.

No media.

No politicians except for the mayor of Rockhampton.

And it would be interesting how the mayor turned up.

If the greenies were trying to infiltrate, they would be the first to be picked up by Bonnie and Clyde as they were the only people that never washed and stank. Even Bonnie and Clyde would turn their noses up at them and hide their eyes, barking a little.

To have this momentous occasion, the castle grounds needed to be safe, Alfred made sure of that.

Amounts to them all came Ikav and his family, Drew and family, Ernie and family, the supervisor for D crew Gerry Buyers and Trevor Keen. Yes, Trevor turned up and made the effort to stay sober and not have any alcohol with him.

You wouldn't recognise these people at first because of their fancy dress.

Ikav—with wife, daughter, and son—came as a highland tribesman of Papua New Guinea.

Drew came dressed as Elvis with the big side burns, his wife dressed as Dolly Parton.

There were the few guests who went a little hysterical as there was an Elvis sighting.

Ernie was dressed as the Terminator and of course he kept mimicking Arnie, "I'll be back." It seemed a little repetitious for a while but Ernie soon got sick of saying it and went on to mimic something else of Arnie's.

Fortunately no one was dressed as a miner, as that had been stipulated in the registrations as being a no no.

The Nandi executive was on his way in the helicopter with his staff of three. Gert had the pad ready for the landing, and he would await the chopper in his hi vis dress, standing clear of the big Red Cross on the helipad. Once landed, he would escort the four personnel to where the function was being held.

The last guests had arrived, the stone mason gang in their Fred Flintstone and Barney Rubble attire, which made quite an impression for their age. And of course the neighbours on either side of the castle.

Then there was a surprise last guest. Everyone watching couldn't believe he had been let through security in his condition. Only a few knew who he was and what his purpose was in Alfred's castle. There were plenty of awards going to be handed out this Saturday night.

As the afternoon moved on, the awaited ride on mower race was getting organised. Of course Alfred held the checked flag.

By this time now the helicopter with company executive and his staff had landed and Girt was leading them down the stairwell to Alfred and Margareta's picture party. The games were about to begin with Alfred's lawns getting mown at the same time. Once again, a win win for Alfred and everyone attending the function.

In lane one, we had Trevor Keen. Oh yes, the toilet roll king.

In lane two, we had Mad Mike Miller, the fitter who could

break a steel bar without even trying.

In lane three, Hannibal Hector. The man always on the move with a big smile and no teeth.

In lane four, Ikav was going to give it a go in his highland dress, hoping his grass attire would not get ripped off, being caught in the blade cutter with power on.

In lane five, we had Cross-Eyed Flynn the Irishman who would always say and I quote, "To be sure, to be sure, to be sure." Couldn't understand that when he was crosseyed. He did manage to drive a car, so there must be some way he sees straight.

In lane six, we had The Great Dane. He could talk someone into anything, if they saw something in it for themselves. He was focused.

In lane seven, we had Steady Eddy. Give him a job to do and he would upgrade to his own specifications. It was important that Eddy was not given access to the ride ons as he would have modified them. Here everyone gets a fair deal.

In lane eight, we had The Hurricane. Start him, turn your back, and he would be gone, "FOOM," like a hurricane.

In lane nine, we have Two Tonne Gerry. Nice fella, ate a lot on the job whilst working and could be mistaken for a crane driver.

In lane ten, Girt the German tourist was asked to fill the gap to pretend he was Michael Schumacher, having brought the company executive and his staff down to the race.

How is Michael doing? Last time we heard, he was involved in a serious accident.

All ten riders were seatbelted onto their ride ons, engines started, throttles idling, each rider with their D crew helmets on, every ride on had been checked. They were all turbocharged the same. There were no irregularities and it would be up to the individual drivers' skills that would make or break the race to be the winner. The prize was the "GUM BOAT" award and the winners' fundraiser going to charity. Each rider had the task of positioning his own blade to the level he thought adequate. This was the only skill apart from getting their speeds up to cross the finish line on the return part of the strip. Yes, up then down. It would be the skills of the best rider who would take the award.

"Gentlemen, start your engines," called Alfred.

But Alfred, haven't they got their engines idling? Alfred had seemed to have forgotten this.

Holding the flag up, Alfred proceeded to move the checked flag to the down position. The race was on. They were off with a roar and mower blades churning.

What Alfred didn't realise was that he may not have any lawn left. Cross-Eyed Flynn started down the lawn. He would be the first competitor to stall, having carved up great chunks of lawn, and that he did.

Then Mad Mike Miller didn't take too kindly with Hannibal Hector next to him with a smile on his face and no teeth pushing in front of him, so he decided to ram him from behind, pushing him sideways into the wall. Another competitor out.

So there was now Mad Mike Miller and Trevor Keen who was zig zagging not to be intimidated by the Great Dane, as well as Ikav, who was cool and calm and moving in a straight path for the first three hundred meters.

Then came Steady Eddy and the Hurricane, it was as though the Hurricane wanted to fly over the top of Eddy. He certainly was in a hurry, racing toward the first three hundred meters.

Then there was Two-Tonne Gerry, whose weight had nearly exceeded the weight of the ride on and even with the turbo, it wasn't enough to get to the 60km/mph speed.

It now was a race between the German Girt, Steady Ernie, the Great Dane, Trevor Keen, The Hurricane, Mad Mike Miller and Ikav.

The Hurricane and Steady Eddie had managed to spin themselves round in a tyre jack, facing each other and being hooked on to each other.

By this time the guests were roaring with laughter, Alfred's prized lawn was disappearing by the minute and a red-faced Alfred was looking on.

Ikav was moving along quite fast without a care in the world and reaching the three-hundred-meter mark when he suddenly got T-boned on the turn by Mad Mike Miller.

Now they were down to the German Girt who was racing like he was on the track, turning now at the three-hundred-meter mark, with the Great Dane and Trevor Keen in pursuit.

The Great Dane was pointing at something on Trevor Keen's wheel. With his mind fixed, without realising it, Trevor drifted off and went straight into the wall. Trevor then was out of the game.

It was now down to the Great Dane and Girt.

Girt was weaving to and fro in front of the Great Dane. The Great Dane, now up on two wheels, had pulled up alongside Girt to race to the finishing line. The blades were still cutting only so slightly as they had been raised and then came the bang. The Great Dane had blown a piston with smoke pouring out. He had come to a complete stop.

The guests were roaring with laughter. Even the company executive let down his guard and joined in the fun.

That meant the German would cross the finishing line with the checkered flag waved by Alfred, taking the "Gum Boot" award. The presentation would be later in the evening.

Across the lawn were all these damaged and burnt-out relics of ride ons and with close inspection, Alfred's lawn had gone from luscious green grass to big burn out areas and no grass with holes. Not quite what Alfred expected. The game of riding lawnmowers now to mow Alfred's lawn was over for any futuristic cause. Alfred would have to hire someone to mow his lawns if he wasn't going to be home, and of course after he had repaired the dugout holes and burn out areas and replanting. For Alfred now, he realised D crew had made this into a demolition derby.

This was one of the fun parts for the afternoon. The guests would go away talking about the ride on race for weeks to come.

Next on the programme would be the fireworks at dusk. The meals had been prepared and overseen by Margareta and she had got her wish with homegrown meat, fresh road kill and fish of the day with all the other supplements that made the buffet.

The music in the background was being played with orchestral accompaniment. It had been a great day so far. But the ragged guest was still a mystery. Why had Alfred overlooked him? Did Alfred and security feel sorry for him? This was the mystery and only later in the evening would his disguise be revealed.

After the evening meal, the fireworks had been set up away from the approach path into Rockhampton airport and then the presentations would take place on the south side lawn.

The ride on mower competitors had got themselves cleaned up and were going over the event with a few laughs. Apart from demolishing Alfred's lawns and damaging literally every ride on at speed, no one was injured. Just a little ego damaged but that was the intention.

He would get over the holes and burn outs in his law.

Alfred's mind is like a web browser: nineteen tabs are open, three are frozen and he has no idea where the music is coming from.

LET THE SHOW BEGIN

The music played while the lighting affect over the castle walls was magnifying the different colours. There came an announcement over the PA system that the fireworks were going to take place on the eastern side of the castle walls in the next ten minutes.

What had Alfred prepared for his guests? And what was being prepared for Alfred outside the castle?

There were some unhappy people on the other side of the moat. Let's see what happens as the fireworks take place.

Alfred had friends who could organise a thrilling display of fireworks and he had set them up in an area away from where the guests would be.

The countdown came and for the unfortunate crows hanging around the walls of the castle scavenging, it would not be a happy ending.

"Ten, nine, eight, seven, six, five, four, three two, one. BOOM, BOOM, BANG," The display had begun. Then came the thump, thump. Four unfortunate crows came falling.

As the fireworks continued on the eastern side of the castle, the greenies who were trying to infiltrate Alfred's castle were getting bombarded with more crow corpses. Alfred, without realising it, was getting rid of unwanted birds, and bombing the greenies at the same time. This wasn't going down well with the greenies and they were figuring other ways to get back at Alfred and his castle.

Meanwhile, Alfred's guests were continuing to enjoy the display, which lasted for over an hour.

The air traffic was well clear of the fireworks and the castle had become a GPS reference point for aircraft on the approach, who could see a well lit up castle. There had been no complaints from the Rockhampton air traffic control tower or the Civil Aviation Safety Authority, so Alfred must be doing something right. But the best was yet to come. The presentations and the mystery guest.

As everyone, now including the Nandi Chief Executive and his staff, were settling in on the seating arrangement, Alfred called up the guest speaker. To everyone's surprise, a ragged old man in rough clothes approached the speaker's platform. The guests went quiet and then as the ragged old looking man got up to speak, Alfred got up, shook the man's hand and said, "Please welcome the mayor of Rockhampton."

The old shrunken man stood up, composed himself, brushed his hair and said, "You did ask me to come in fancy dress, Alfred."

Then the guests started laughing.

Alfred's neighbours and the stonemasons started dancing on the tables. Alfred thought he was going to have a coronary on his hands and would have to call an ambulance as five senior citizens had been let loose after they had thought it was a hilarious joke about the mayor.

Alfred's night at the castle was getting better by the hour.

Then came the THUD, THUD on the drawbridge door. It kept coming and would not stop. As the mayor continued to speak to the guests and thank Alfred for his large amount of support for the community and the environment over the last fifteen or so years, Alfred and Girt went up the stairwell to investigate what the thud was.

The Greenies. They just couldn't help themselves. Who was paying them this time to make a disturbance and vandalise his drawbridge? It could be one of five organisations that had a vendetta against Alfred.

It wouldn't be the environmentalists as they were like the greenies, not smart and didn't have enough money.

Wouldn't be the council as the mayor was here and he wasn't an informer in Alfred's eyes.

Wouldn't be the banking corporation as they had shut up shop when they looked stupid at not seeing Alfred through with a loan.

There was only one other organisation that Alfred had taken advantage of and robbed them of customers who they themselves had robbed first.

Yes. The power supply authority. Alfred had beaten them at their own game and produced power on a commercial level or maybe a private level for the surrounding neighbours. His hydro station was generating enough electrical capacity on a very cheap rate to put money back into his neighbours' pockets. The power company didn't like that. To get back using any means possible, the greens were there first choice. So the stone throwing had begun and they started throwing rocks at the drawbridge, trying to cause some disturbances.

Alfred had an idea. "Girt, how many crocodiles have we trapped today?"

"*Is es sech,*" replied Girt in German.

"Six it is," said Alfred. "I think they are hungry enough by now."

As it was dark outside the castle and the waters of the moat were quite calm, Alfred and Girt raced down to the under waters of the castle, where they had trapped the six three-meter-long crocs, and let four of them out. In the morning, Alfred would be handing over the two remaining crocodiles to the environmentalists.

"Hopefully this will keep the noise down a bit, Alfred."

At least the rocks weren't fired from catapults with burning tar as they did in the medieval times, Alfred thought. Then Alfred thought again to himself, *The greenies wouldn't be smart enough to construct something like a catapult.*

The rocks kept being fired at the drawbridge like trajectories for the next half hour and then it all stopped.

Alfred and Girt had made it back to the gathering and were back joining in the festivities.

Alfred didn't mind the rain.
He had a smile to hide any pain

and Alfred always dreams of things to do
with always one hundred dollars stuck in his shoe.
There'll be no load of compromisin'
as victory was on the horizon.
He's gonna be where the lights are shining on him.

And that's where Alfred went back to, his guests.

The mayor had just cracked some funny jokes to keep the guests amused when he turned his head and saw Alfred and Girt coming towards him.

The mayor started to applaud Alfred and guests got up to clapping.

As the clapping stopped, the mayor spoke a few words.

"Well, Alfred, you and Margareta have certainly excelled yourselves so far today with all the entertainment, even the fitting music, the food, and the costumed guests. Alfred, a number of these guests are from D crew with company executive and staff?"

Alfred nodded.

"And your neighbours and other invited guests, welcome. I apologise for my attire, but Alfred, you did say come as a mystery guest, so I hope it hasn't offended too many people. I don't dress like this on a normal work day."

Then everyone laughed.

"Just a few words I would like to say," said the mayor. "Alfred's castle has become an attraction for the area and we hope will be opened to the public. Thanks once again, Alfred and Margareta, for the invite. I'll hand you over to Alfred now to say a few words."

There was a clap in response to the mayor's little speech.

"Is everyone having a good time?" called Alfred.

"Yes," came the reply.

"Well, apart from my lawns being demolished and a few wrecked ride ons, we have come to that part of the evening for the award presentations, followed by the pool opening. I hope everyone brought their swimming gear or else a few people will be going home in their wet clothes."

Everyone laughed a bit harder.

"Just a few housekeeping requirements," said Alfred. "Everyone is welcome to be shown around the castle. There will be those guests who are staying over, a room has been allocated for you. Any unruly guests we have downstairs accommodation in the dungeon."

Everyone laughed.

"We have also had some disturbances from some unwanted guests outside the castle, we think we now have it under control, but please, when anyone leaves the castle grounds tonight, do not feel intimidated, the security will be on watch," said Alfred.

At that point Alfred handed over the podium to the Chief Executive for Nandi, David MacDonald.

"Thanks, Alfred, for the invite to your pool party. Must say, Alfred, we have been following your ideas and input into the company's reputation, from castle building to bobsledding. Who else would have come up with these weird ideas and got a team together? Impressive," said David McDonald.

"Now we are going to have some fun with the presentations," said David. "Firstly, we have four runners-up. Napoleon, Muhammad Ali, Wonder Woman, Kenny Rogers. Got to remind you if the winner is a singer, he has to sing a song from the performer he has chosen."

David gave the envelope to Julie his secretary.

"The winner in tonight's fancy dress is none other than Elvis," called Julie.

Drew, who had been dressed as Elvis, came up to the podium. Indeed there had been an Elvis sighting. It was at Alfred's castle and the guests were clapping and whistling.

Just as Elvis would have said to the crowd, so did Drew: "Thank you very much, thank you very much."

Once the guests had quietened, a small speech of appreciation to Alfred as his friend and a friend to many.

The stringed sextet was ready to play the accompaniment of an Elvis number. They and the guests waited in anticipation to see what noise was going to come out of Drew's mouth and would it have any resemblance to the voice of Elvis.

Drew had been watching Alfred over those months when he would greet the sunrise with his ukulele and sing on the mine site where no one could hear him except for the three seated, Drew happened to be one of the three. He saw Alfred's determination to extend those vocal cords to sing along without everyone having to shut their ears to a terrible noise. So Drew too went home and practiced without anyone knowing, not even his wife, and here he was impersonating an Elvis song or two, which in respect he did know the words. So Drew would give it a go.

Drew got up in his white Elvis suit. In a deep voice, he said, "I've decided to sing 'Love me tender, love me sweet.'"

Wasn't sure if Drew meant this for his wife or Alfred, but he decided to sing it. All the ladies were taking out their hankies crying. Even Alfred had a tear in his eye.

Then to get the orchestral sextet going, Drew finished with "Moody Blues."

Well, it's hard to be a miner
bettin' on a banger
That changes ev'ry time.
Well, you think you're gonna run.
Think she's givin' him a look.
A stranger's all you find.
Yeah, it's hard to understand
what she's yelling about.

That she's a woman as we know.
She's a complicated lady,
so colour my lady moody blue.
Oh, moody blue.
Tell me, does it get to you?

I keep hangin' in
try to learn a new song
but it never happens.
Oh moody blue.

The guests went wild. Fred Flintstone and Barney Rubble went into dancing mode, dancing on the table. Elvis had been gone forty-three years and now he had been reborn. Two ninety-three-year-old men dancing prolifically.

Alfred was getting a little worried when he saw that. An ambulance might need to be on standby for any cardiac arrests. But for the rest of the guests, this was getting better by the hour.

For the stringed sextet, they were in their element at this time of night. All the crows had been scared away and the kookaburras could be heard in the background, making a few noises.

When Drew had finished his Elvis impersonations and the encore made, it was time for the awards to be presented for the great ride on mower race. Coming to present the "Gum Boot" award was the Chief Executive for Nandi mining, David MacDonald.

"Well, wasn't that great. Even miners can have a talent to sing. Maybe we will have the three tenors singing soon." David laughed. "Alfred's given me this presentation for the ride on race, as he is still getting over his demolished lawn."

Everyone laughed. Even Alfred.

"But I would like to present this award on behalf of a charity we support to the good German, Girt Hoffman. Ladies and gentlemen, this young man has the makings of a Michael Schumacher. Maybe Michael started off riding on mowers first."

Everyone laughed again.

It was a momentous occasion for Girt as he had never won anything in his life, and to win the first and last "Gum Boot" award was a thrill. He thanked his competitors who were looking on, especially Cross-Eyed Flynn who was seeing two of Girt. Alongside him was the Great Dane as the runner up to Girt. It was all fun as Girt put it, with male egos put aside it, was hilarious.

Girt said a few words at the podium.

"Ja mein name ist girt, und ich mochte mir vor allem Alfred und Margareta fur die moglichhkeit der arbeit hier bedanken, diesen tag zum erfolg zu machen. Vielen dank."

If you don't know what that means, it is simply, "Yes, my name is Girt, and I would like to thank Alfred and Margareta for the opportunity of work here to make this day a success. Thank you."

There was applause, a few hoots from D crew and a few laughs.

Alfred then shook Girt's hand and got up to the podium and spoke, as the final entertainment for the evening was the pool party. No one had seen the pool in all its glory yet.

"This part of the evening will be the mystery unveiled and I couldn't have done it without the help of my two closest neighbours, Albert Einstein Junior with his wife Gertrude, who installed in me the law of relativity, as Alfred used this on practical terms to build their brick wall and the closest neighbour on the other side, Thomas Edison Junior, that had given Alfred practical advice on designing stuff," said Alfred.

After a few more light refreshments, Alfred ushered all the guests into the pool complex area.

There weren't many castles around with a pool complex. A lap pool lit up in the colours of the rainbow and would change colours with use of a timer. The orchestral sextet began playing Handel's Water Music followed by a little Mozart music.

"Now," said Alfred. "Everyone is invited to have a dunk in the water. There is a water slide for those adventurous types, but please don't knock yourselves out coming down it. There is a midnight toast to the evening also."

Now as soon as Alfred had said these words, a helicopter started buzzing around over the castle with an intentional search light, shining straight into Alfred's guests' eyes.

The Greenies again, thought Alfred. "The greenies, Girt, what have we got to shoot their lights out with?" called Alfred. "They cannot be more than a thousand feet high to annoy us with those searchlights."

Girt had mentioned he had been a sniper in the German Armed forces and could practically take anything out within a thousand yards.

"Girt, I have a spud gun mounted on a tripod, you reckon you could take the light out, quickly reload, and stun a few greenies? They will be hovering for awhile overhead, trying to intimidate us at the pool complex. Tripod is mounted and it's gassed," said Alfred.

"*Lass uns girt gehen*, let's go," called Girt.

These greenies will stop at nothing that's good for the community and bad for them, thought Alfred. *Let's give them something so they have nothing to work with.*

"Can I have your attention quickly, please?" called Alfred to his guests. "We have one more display for you whilst you finish off the evening enjoying the pool complex. We have been given the task of reducing the helicopter's search lights over us."

Everyone was thinking what had Alfred planned to finish the entire evening off. Those lights were so bright and glared from that chopper.

Meanwhile, Alfred and Girt had raced into position near the helicopter pad on the first castle landing.

Positioning themselves within range of the hovering helicopter, Girt took aim within one hundred yards and fired a cannon full of spuds at high impact. A direct hit took out one search light. Before the greenies knew what hit them, Girt had taken another blast of the cannon, taking out a second search light as the helicopter turned, hitting one of the greenies in the chest. One more shot quickly smashed through the side of the helicopter.

The crowd by now were a bit high on the celebrations and were cheering.

It was time for another song to finish off the evening. The greenies were not seen again that night. Damages to an aircraft would be reported to the Civil Aviation Safety Authority but one thing Alfred had in his favour, none of the greenies knew where or what was fired on them as the impact of the potatoes once demolishing the lights and the side of the helicopter would have disintegrated.

Alfred and Girt came down to the pool complex. This time round there were guests in the pool, there were some now in their birthday suites.

Alfred thought his streaking days were left at the camp, but apparently some of D crew had cottoned on and decided to try it out for themselves.

"ELVIS, ELVIS, ELVIS," the guests kept chanting.

Drew was called up again for one more song.

"Okay, okay," said Drew. "One more."

Drew walked over to the stringed sextet and asked them to play.

"I'm going to sing 'Wise men say.'"

There was an applause by the guests.

"Here we go," called Drew, as the music rolled, microphone in his hand.

The guests were cheering and clapping as the evening was coming to a close.

There were a few very tired guests and their rooms were waiting for them.

Alfred had made one more closing announcement and then said if anyone wishes to continue partying into the early hours of the morning, the pool facilities would remain open.

One good thing, no one could get drunk as there was no alcohol through the night, only drinks with no alcohol content in them with some alcohol beverage tastes. What a good trick Alfred played on his guests or was it just cost cutting measure? It probably was a bit of both. But this did minimise any possible drownings.

The night had been a success and would be remembered by all for some time. The cleaning up would be helped by Margareta and her young tourist staff. One of the young German girls, Ingrid, although just a friend to Girt, had taken a real shine to him, he was her hero. She had not known any of his background as he had never talked about it. Long hair and a beard had disguised all that. Tonight he had shown some of that secret background on three separate occasions. He had served well with Alfred and would come highly recommended if he did decide to leave Alfred and Margareta's employment.

What stunned Girt: Where did Alfred get all the money from to build all this? Did Alfred come from a rich family? Had he inherited some millions? Had he invested in something that exploded into huge dividends? What was his secret? Did the mines pay him generously or had he cashed in his life's savings? Girt was a bit reluctant to ask but he felt like he had to know.

The castle was modelled off a Bavarian castle back in Europe which he knew well as he had been inside it as a guest.

No one except wealthy aristocrat families lived in castles that were kept in the family and to maintain them was some considerable cost.

Alfred was planning on a castle village, with an aquatic centre, stalls, training centres and, yes, a postal service. Inside a castle no one would know what was going on compared to a central hub or village outside. What's in the castle stays in the castle were Alfred's words. So really, he Alfred and Margareta had a small kingdom of their own.

Those that never took Alfred seriously were beginning to regret that now as he could only go from strength to strength and he had a backing of the mayor of Rockhampton, his neighbours who Alfred did look after, D crew, his working colleagues who were now able to use Alfred's castle for family retreats on request. What was so bad about that?

But Alfred would always be a target for jealous and socialistic people. One good thing about Alfred, not saying he is limited to one good thing, Alfred didn't care what people thought. He put the work in other people wouldn't do, Alfred dreamed up ideas and treated them as goals to aim for. Alfred also respected others' decisions but also would want to get his point across.

If you ever meet Alfred, you will find he carries a notebook around with him. If an idea comes to mind, he will write it down. Mind you, if it's a good idea not a stupid idea. One of his best ideas so far was setting up his own crypto currency, making false money the banks use to build, and then buying real money silver and gold. Reserves that would come in handy in the near future and only Alfred and Margareta would know where these treasures were hidden. Yes, planning for the future was as good as it gets.

What things can we learn from Alfred because of the pool party?

When things don't go to plan, don't get mad.

When certain organisations annoy and start damaging property, find a way get rid of them.

Make your plans inspiring for others to enjoy.

Bring a sense of mystery to any event and make it humorous. This was certainly Alfred all over.

Everyone is different and everyone has got something to bring to the table, as Alfred would say.

Alfred decided to give everyone interested a tour of the castle and some of its secrets from the downstairs to the very top of the castle that looks over the Pacific Ocean to the solar panel power generation, to overlooking the lit hydro power station.

Alfred decided to show a few hidden passages and where they led, but not all of them. There were the workers' quarters, the machinery and vehicle storage, the kitchens. The bathrooms. Some areas Alfred was still working on.

"Alfred, where do you get the time and energy to do all this and the finance, when you're away seven days at a time?"

"Check the crypto currency markets for a start," said Alfred, "and look at the horses I bet on. Some of them I have bought with winnings. See the hydro dam, guess who pays for cheap power. And yes, I have enemies as well. See what happened tonight."

It wasn't all easygoing for Alfred, as some weeks he turned up to work sleep deprived. His colleagues would have to cover for his fatigue management with cardboard replicas.

"New plans for the village stores, aquatic centre, information centre and a private chapel, once I get more crypto sorted, and of course back to work Tuesday."

It was now in the early hours of Sunday morning, with a lot of sleep deprivation by those who stayed overnight. It would seem like a morning of snoozing for them, but not for King Alfred.

He had made it a routine that early every Sunday morning, he would be in his chapel, just being thankful for life, friends, health, and family. Alfred's crazy ideas were what made his friends and colleagues respect him, as the weekend had shown. There was not one of his guests there that had not made an effort to come. Some had travelled four to eight hours to make an appearance. That's how respected Alfred was. A team effort by D crew.

The stone masons, well, they had seen their last work, had a sense of achievement, revisited Elvis, rocked their last song, re-lived the Flintstones error. What more could they have asked for at their age? They were driven home by taxi that night and were found the next day. Both had passed away with a smile on their faces.

The neighbours now believed Alfred was a man of his word and someone they could count on, a confidante, a man's man. Walking home that night, they were never intimidated as security escorted them. The greenies were in hiding. Or were they just waiting?

What Alfred had not found out yet was that in the midst of re-leasing the crocs the night before to ward off the greenies, they had tried to barricade his drawbridge and stop it from opening. They must have tried to do this as a last resort after those guests who had left and security was brought back into the castle when the drawbridge was brought up. The greenies had managed to secure steel poles to wedge the drawbridge shut, but what they weren't smart enough to figure out, the weight of a ten-ton drawbridge, gravity and a high-powered electric motor would either bend or punch the poles into the ground. The matter was dealt with quickly before the rest of the guests left the castle that day. The Chief Executive of Nandi and his staff had also decided to take Alfred and Margareta up on his offer to stay overnight and fly out with the pilot the next day. The pilot had been in the background taking in all that happened over the weekend. He had commented to his boss that this was one of the most fun weekends he had had in a long time.

There had also been a complaint made to the Civil Aviation Safety Authority about damages and safety to a helicopter from the night before. The facts had not been given, as in the darkness no one on board the helicopter had seen where the trajectories had come from. This complaint still had to be noted as safety was involved. If forensics got involved, all they would find was decomposing potatoes imbedded into the helicopter panels, insinuating a spud gun had been used. Of course no one would ever admit to this if questioned.

Smart thinking once again by Alfred and Girt. Girt too was becoming a very hands-on man. And whilst Alfred was working his tour of duty, Girt would now be the protector and advisor to security for the castle.

So from refuelling generators, heavy vehicles, fixing vehicles, breaking vehicles to building castles and power networks, it was clear Alfred was on his way to being a consultant before retiring as a professional bobsledder in the future.

The day was fast approaching when Alfred would have to board the mining charter aircraft for work with his work colleagues. This week would be the weekend talk in pre start. But before they could get to pre start, another event was going to take place.

THE AIRCRAFT INCIDENT

The taxi that Tuesday afternoon had come to pick Alfred up to drop him off at Rockhampton Airport.

There was nothing unusual about that.

Alfred was in the final stages of a bullet sized prototype bob-sled under patent. Alfred had been thinking about this on the way to the airport. Every one of his colleagues seemed happy. It was just another work day. The pilot had debriefed everyone before boarding. This was a single engine turbine aircraft that carried twelve people. Every second week, this company flew staff on day shift and it had a good reputation.

Everyone had been screened for that dreaded covid and boarding would commence within minutes.

Alfred had been the talk of the crew. The ride on race, the fireworks display, the fancy dress and Elvis, the search light shoot outs and the pool party with music. Every one of the crew were just shaking their heads in amazement. Some if not all had shared on social media; the likes were phenomenal. Everyone was happy.

But this one day, the pilot flying the aircraft looked in good health, nothing out of the ordinary.

Having sat around for an hour, it was time for boarding. Alfred had taken his seat next to Drew and Ernie. The doors were closed and the generator was cranking the turbine engine as it was winding up. With a taxi clearance, the aircraft would be soon on the main runway with a clearance and an altitude level for Nandi mine. The pilot had inserted the GPS setting on the screen with a distance and allocated time to destination.

Alfred was sitting next to his pilot friend who worked as a fitter at Nandi mine, he wasn't the pilot flying the aircraft though, just a passenger. He had not been able to attend Alfred's party due to a family engagement prior. He suffered the disappointment, having heard what Alfred had been up to over the weekend. But thems were the breaks.

Alfred had often asked Leigh Roy what happens if the only pilot loses consciousness or becomes incapacitated for some reason in flight. It was a good question and with quick thinking, Alfred would quietly say, "We take over, flying in the right-hand seat."

"Has this ever happened to you, Leigh Roy?" asked Alfred.

"No, but there is always a first time," came the reply.

"Well, let's hope it doesn't happen here," Alfred said quietly.

Alfred had spoken a little too soon as within half an hour being in the air and the plane on auto pilot, the pilot slumped over the controls, unconscious. The boys down the back hadn't seen this happen as many had their eyes closed, sleeping. Alfred and Leigh Roy certainly did.

"Alfred, the pilot's unconscious, we got to turn the aircraft round and head back. Can you hold the pilot back to stop him slumping over the controls?"

Alfred thought for a minute and ripped his belt off without thinking about it. They nearly had two catastrophes, the unconscious pilot and Alfred caught with his pants down. The pilot came first, tying him back into his seat.

"What's going on?" Some of the "D" Crew had started to wake up.

"Just got a slight problem, Ernie," said Alfred in a calm voice.

"What sort of a problem?" Ernie called with a concerned voice.

"We've just changed pilots and we are turning the aircraft back to Rocky," Alfred said very calmly.

"Who's flying the plane, Alfred?" Drew called out.

"Leigh Roy."

The plane went silent.

There was some panic.

"We are going down," called another "D" Crew member.

Alfred at this point knew just what to do. The famous Alfred slap across the face came to a nearly hysterical Herman.

Leigh Roy had gained control of the aircraft, turned round, and set heading back to Rocky. He had called the tower, advising of the emergency situation and stating he would land the turbine single engine aircraft.

Meanwhile, the pilot was held back in his seat with his safety belt on and partially Alfred's belt to keep him upright. There were only a few times Alfred was caught with his pants down and this was one of them. To hold them up as best he could, on this occasion, as it was a mining charter, he had a couple of spare cable ties in his carry-on bag in case of emergencies. On a commercial flight carrying things as cable ties is a no no.

Leigh Roy had successfully turned the plane around, setting a heading on a reciprocal GPS track to Rockhampton, maintaining his height. The Rockhampton tower had called an emergency and emergency vehicles were on standby.

The unconscious pilot was strapped in, Alfred had recovered from the short fall of his pants, cable ties came in handy. The D crew passengers had recovered from a state of shock, as Alfred had slapped it out of them, and the plane was going to land safely. Wasn't that a good result?

Leigh Roy was in his element.

Although the outcome would be good, Alfred broke one of his first rules. Don't get caught with your pants down.

The single engine turbine was on a descent into Rockhampton airport. The emergency services were on standby. There was an announcement that a pilot was in a serious condition and had lost consciousness. But who was flying the aircraft?

Leigh Roy had been talking to the Rockhampton tower nonstop. He had figured out the engine performance and power settings. He had switched off the auto pilot, flying manually, and was continually monitoring the fuel levels. Fortunately, the sky was clear as making an instrument approach in cloud would have been at the controller's mercy as there were no approach plates visible from the pilot's seat.

Just to put a spanner in the works, Leigh Roy couldn't resist saying this over the PA system:

"Ladies and gentlemen, this is your captain speaking. We are about to commence our descent into Rockhampton airport. We ask you take your allocated seats with seatbelts on."

Leigh Roy turned to Alfred and said, "How good was that?"

Meanwhile, the unconscious pilot was making some groaning noises. Every one of D crew in the seats behind were quiet as a mouse, hanging on to their seats with their eyes closed.

For Alfred, this was another day in the life. Fortunately Leigh Roy knew exactly what was expected of him, but what everyone on the ground was not expecting, Leigh Roy was going to do: a fly past and go around and land. In Leigh Roy's eyes, he just wanted to get comfortable with the plane in case he had to do this all over again.

For the emergency services on the ground, this was not a good idea. They had been called in for an emergency for a crash landing.

"Everyone buckle in, show time," said Leigh Roy.

"DELTA 252, you cleared for finals runway 33, Wind 010 M 10KTS. Emergency vehicles on standby to give assistance," came the call from the tower.

Leigh Roy deliberately came in too high and requested to make a go around. The controllers in the tower noted that Leigh Roy was coming in too high, not realising it was deliberate.

"DELTA 252, you coming in too high, too fast."

"DELTA 252 going around to make another approach."

Leigh Roy kept the speed up, flying at 130kts till he cleared the end of runway 33 and climbed back up to one thousand feet. They levelled off in the circuit to make a second approach, emergency aircraft having right of way over all other aircraft.

The controllers on watch knew this guy could fly but nobody knew who he was except just one of the mining staff.

Every one of the crew were only anxious to get back on the ground. The pilot himself was Alfred and Leigh Roy's concern now. He had started to make more noises of regaining consciousness, a good sign.

Leigh called the tower on base for runway 33.

"Delta 252 turning finals."

"Delta 252 cleared to land. Ambulance on standby. Taxi to the terminal."

The landing was a perfect three-point landing, and then Leigh Roy applied power on the brakes. Leigh Roy turned and backtracked towards the taxiway, where emergency services were waiting. Everyone from D crew clamped and applauded Leigh Roy and Alfred for the team effort. Twelve lives had been spared by two men's quick thinking and removing a personal belt.

The aircraft came to a standstill. Leigh Roy shut the turbine down, and as soon as the engine stopped, the ambulance arrived to get the pilot out, its first priority.

The back door was opened and the Rocky members of D crew quickly got out.

Leigh Roy and Alfred were ushered away to be debriefed on the whole incident by the company that owned the aircraft and the Civil Aviation Safety Authority. It was a little upsetting for members of D crew. However, most, if not all, D crew were not hesitant to get back on a single engine turbine knowing that Alfred and Leigh Roy had their backs as a second pilot. If Alfred was there, things would always be okay. So the story of the day would be told again for weeks to come. Another flight would be organised by the other charter company that flew into Nandi. D crew had to be checked out medically, as this had been a trauma. If they were flown out an hour later, it would be just on civil twilight. That was ok as there was runway lighting not toilet roll lighting. But company policy for safety's sake and the men's emotions, fly out would be tomorrow.

Leigh Roy and Alfred would follow a day later, as company policy, they would be making a statement. Oh, how Alfred liked writing reports. He was a real colourful writer.

This time around, Leigh Roy and Alfred would get an award.

THE COMPLETION
OF THE BOBSLED

It had been a long ten months with the secrecy of the bobsled project.

Flying in a day later meant people and workable equipment would have been held up for twenty-four hours. Still Alfred had got there. Alfred had gone home for an extra day after the aircraft incident. When Alfred did return the following day, the company had forwarded an email to his supervisor giving the highest approval ever for validation and confirmation of Nandi support not only to represent them internationally through advertising in the Olympic bobsled tournament but to be the company's ambassador for promoting its products and reserves as well.

Big responsibility, Alfred. Could this be the making or breaking of Alfred? He would never confide in anyone except that one person, that one special person. We will find out later.

Alfred hadn't known till recently, Nandi mining had put out a tender for the building of new maintenance, stores, and heavy vehicle workshops. In that location, a new facility for experimental equipment had been drawn up. Was Alfred's cover for the bobsled and team a cover for something else in Nandi mining interest? There was something else out there in the ground that needed to be kept under secret. Only time would tell and Alfred might be that person who unlocks that secret without even knowing it.

Why had Nandi mining been interested in sponsoring a bobsled team who were building the team from scratch and a new designed lightweight high speed machine? Alfred was going to find this out in the not-so-distant future. What was so special about this bobsled fabrication? In the meantime the training, the physical and mental endurance the team was going through, was going to plan.

The finished and furnished machine would be transported to a ready-made track south of Mackay, and the team with the bobsled would be going through its trials there for the next month. The team with the bobsled would have to go through vigorous tests and this would be on wheels as there was no snow. There would be a month of vigorous training following the next swing and each member would be paid to take that four weeks off.

The big question running through Alfred's mind: *What is so important to Nandi mining that they are pouring everything, no matter what it costs, into this project?*

Alfred always knew most sponsorships worked on a budget. But Nandi never had a budget, it seemed. So what were they hiding?

What is so important about this particular bobsled? Alfred thought.

For Alfred, trying to keep priorities in check, this required careful planning. The fuel carts still had to be managed, the pit was getting deeper and more heavy earth moving machines were on the circuit. The workshop machinery and vehicle parts had to be ordered. There were meetings to attend and on top of all that, Margareta, back at the castle with the staff, was still trying to keep the greenies at bay and was ringing Alfred every night he was away to get his thoughts on the matter.

Alfred reminded himself once again, "When the going gets tough, the tough get going."

Alfred was also reminding himself as he had always reminded others to, "Always think on the bright side of life de dum, de dum, de dum dedum dedum!"

Everyone on D decree except the riders were wondering what was going on now. Everything had been kept a secret for so long with the bobsled project. What started out as a joke had become something very serious and Alfred was in the middle of it all with a team of six. There was Ikav, Drew, Ernie, Trevor Keen, Bob

Nolan, Roger Macfarlane. Alfred was the manager.

Was Alfred now an undercover agent for something really big? He had been promoted pretty fast with all his exploitations on show.

Time would tell. Alfred had also built an immunity to the so-called world virus or plaque that brought great misery on the world. As the team was free of any immediate symptoms, could this also be part of the Nandi experiment on body and soul to show the world, as Nandi produces men of steel?

What did happen though in this swing on at work prior to the month-long bobsled live training was that a fatality nearly happened in the lunch room. Yes, Alfred nearly choked on a large piece of salami. It had lodged in his throat and was nearly choking him. Trying to drink fluid to dislodge it with no avail and going red in the face, Alfred was in distress. Ikav knew immediately what to do. Coming up from behind him, wrapping his arms around Alfred below his stomach, Ikav gave one big heave to force the air up to his throat to try and dislodge the chunk of salami. It slightly dislodged but Alfred still had a little trouble breathing. Ikav tried a second time. One piece of salami dislodged and went flying into Ernie's coffee. A very concerned Ernie had not realised he had some floaties in his drink and would not have noticed if there hadn't been a roar of laughter.

Alfred was nearly dying from a choking episode. Three of his other colleagues joined in to help get Alfred some medical attention. A site emergency was called once again and this time it was for Alfred. This time it wasn't Alfred called up; it was Drew calling up on channel three.

"Emergency, emergency, emergency."

The reply came back.

"What is the nature of your emergency, your name and whereabouts."

"Trevor Keen calling, man choking on a piece of salami in workshop crib, need urgent medical assistance."

Paramedics were on their way.

With Alfred still gasping for breath, big Ikav used the Heimlich method from behind with his strong arms.

Ikav thought, *I am glad Alfred didn't suffer from a cardiac arrest and become unconscious.* He would have had to give Alfred mouth-to-mouth resuscitation. A woman seemed more appealing.

The salami was still stuck in Alfred's throat, but because it had dislodged a little, Alfred was able to breathe with a little discomfort.

This was the third time in three months the RFDS flying doctors might have to be called in, this time for the man who himself had rescued three other members from D crews. This is Alfred the rescuer being rescued.

The paramedics arrived just in time. Ikav was just getting a little tired from continually thrusting on Alfred's stomach to try and dislodge the salami.

"We'll take it from here," the paramedics called as they arrived. "Alfred," called the paramedics. "What have you been up to?"

Alfred kept thinking, *It's very hard taking one breath.*

It happens to the best. You stop singing and your throat gets out of practice. No excuses, Alfred thought. *He had just blown it with a salami.*

"Alfred, stay with me," called the paramedic. "We will have that nasty piece of salami out in no time and give you some clean oxygen to breathe in."

Initially, Alfred was trying to point the paramedics. Something was lodged in his throat. The paramedics were insisting they take Alfred's blood pressure as he was going red in the face.

It was only when Alfred kept pointing to his mouth that he got a response. This is was what the emergency was all about. "Someone choking, that someone was none other than Alfred."

The paramedic grabbed her torch, they then could see an object stuck in Alfred's throat. "Alfred, we are going to have to place you over a chair, face down, and force the air from your stomach upwards to dislodge that salami. You've got to give one big cough as well, Alfred."

Alfred nodded. The area was clear. Ikav, Drew, and Ernie stood by and watched, a little concerned for their friend.

"Ready, Alfred?" called the paramedic. "Here we go, one, two, three."

The air was forced up from Alfred's stomach, Alfred gave a big cough, the salami went flying, at the same time Alfred let off a massive big fart. It echoed all over the crib hut and the aroma was none too pleasant. Doors were let open, as those of Alfred's work colleagues rushed to them.

Fortunately Alfred's bowels did not let loose but it came really close.

"How do you feel, Alfred?" called the paramedic.

A hoarse voice came from Alfred.

"It's as though I had the worst sore throat ever and can breathe properly again."

There was a sigh of relief from Alfred's friend and a cheer. Alfred had made it through once again through a critical issue that nearly ended his life.

"Alfred, the Flying Doctors have been called in to take you through to Townsville hospital for observations on your throat. The doctors have been notified at the hospital and would like to do some checks just to be sure."

All Alfred could think of now was the team. The bobsled team were counting on him to be there at the training program south of Mackay in the next week. Alfred was the planner, coach, and trainer.

The last three months had been the best six months ever. With the completion of his pool, the pool party, building a good relationship with his neighbours, the simultaneous emergencies he was involved in, and I must say he won a civilian award for, and now this. It hurt to talk. All this from a chunk of salami caught in his throat, but this would not discourage Alfred. Salami or no salami, Alfred was going to be there for the training for his bobsled team. They were counting on him, the company was counting on Alfred, and lastly his retirement policy was counting on this significant event.

Margareta had been notified as next of kin of Alfred's choking episode. During the phone call, Margareta burst into tears.

"My Alfred, my Alfred," she cried aloud in Spanish.

The interpreter had to translate into German for the staff, but they could see how upset Margareta was by the news of Alfred's close encounter with a piece of salami had been.

Two of the German girls gave Margareta a big hug and said that Alfred was going to be alright.

"You get on the next plane to Townsville and meet with Alfred and bring him home. We will sort every salami out," cried the young frauline.

It was an emotional moment for Margareta. Her Alfred was being flown out by the RFDS (Royal Flying Doctor Service) to Townsville base hospital. Margareta didn't understand why, but she knew this was something serious for her Alfred. She started to cry even harder.

Margareta packed a few things together when her mind cleared and was driven to Rockhampton airport with her interpreter to board the next available flight to Townsville.

The castle was left in safe hands with her German staff and security, who were now becoming family to her and Alfred.

Alfred, meanwhile, was drinking as much milk as he could get, to ease the harshness the salami had caused to his throat. Alfred had been kept under observation by the paramedics till the doctor arrived, a precaution taken in case Alfred suffered an adverse reaction.

This was just annoying for Alfred as he was fit and healthy, so he thought. Alfred was in the training program for his team, he had never had any ailments, matter of fact he had never taken any experimental drugs many companies were trying to enforce due to a fake pandemic. Alfred and many others as well as the company had seen through all this and were on the rise to some of the fittest and healthiest miners in the country. Alfred would get over this mild hiccup due to a misadventure with a piece of salami. He would do the right thing, be flown to Townsville by RFDS and go through the medical protocols. The upside of it was Alfred had never been on an RFDS flight, though he had sent others out on medical emergencies with the RFDS and now he was on one.

Alfred was informed Margareta was on her way to the Townsville hospital. She had been so upset when the news was broken to her that her Alfred had suffered a heart attack from choking on a piece of Salami. This was Chinese whispers. The story had been enlarged slightly due to an initial incorrect diagnosis by the paramedics. Alfred's blood pressure had been normal through the whole saga although he had gone red in the face. Having been driven to the mining airport and waiting for the RFDS, there was no time for feeling sorry for himself. Alfred was an overcomer.

Alfred was now in the recovery mode; all his vital signs were normal. The RFDS had flown into the Nandi airport and Alfred was given an assessment by the doctor and was asked how he felt.

Alfred couldn't say he was one hundred percent but would fly with the medical team back to Townsville.

Meanwhile Ikav, Drew, Ernie, Trevor Keen, and Roger Macfarlane had nothing but concern for their fearless leader Alfred. They would be kept updated and had been advised he would be back soon.

In the mess hall, salami had been taken off the menu as it could now become a health risk for any other unsuspecting person.

The bobsled team had pledged that month of vigorous training with Alfred and must still go ahead for Alfred and the company who had given them so much support.

There was something about this prototype bobsled Alfred knew about that the team didn't know about. Alfred also was sure the company did not know what he knew about concerning the bobsled.

There was a new alloy-based metal that no one had ever used for racing. It gave the advantage of being very light and strong and would meet any racing standard specifications. This was a trade secret and Alfred had somehow stumbled across the composition details in the build to the bobsled. The company was aware of Chinese industrial espionage and they were not going to let a composition as strong and light as this fall into the wrong hands.

The company over the last year had watched Alfred's very successful and unusual ways of achieving, from simple ideas blown up into large and fantastic ideas. He also had the trust and respect from people around him.

When management had attended Alfred's pool party those two weeks ago, they had taken notes. It wasn't just a party for them, it was a game, also of how Alfred could manage so many people and how he could handle stress.

We know the biggest stress in his life was how to handle Margareta. If he could handle her, there was not much he couldn't handle.

Alfred was helped onto the RFDS Beech King Air, seated and given plenty of fluids.

Alfred had brought up in a pass meeting earlier that day the importance of not getting dehydrated and drinking plenty of fluid, with the Queensland heat. Good point, Alfred. Now that Alfred had been under choking conditions and had lost a lot of fluid, he was actually practicing what he had preached, drinking up large, which also soothed his now sore throat.

The turbines of the King Air spooled into life and a taxi briefing was given by the captain at the uncontrolled mining airport to other oncoming traffic. An HF radio transmission to Brisbane control said that the plane was cleared for take off en route to Townsville.

By the time the RFDS flight would land and taxi to the RFDS base, Margareta would also be there to meet up with Alfred as he would be going through some tests at the hospital.

Back on site, a safety investigation was being initiated. Statements were being taken by D crew personnel on what happened to Alfred and could anything have prevented the accident. What steps could be put in place to prevent another incident like this?

Everyone interviewed came to the same conclusion. The salami was the root cause of Alfred's problems. Would there be a ban on salamis in future?

Just sit right back and hear a tale,
a tale of an accident
that started from mining crib
that involved poor Alfred's lunch.

Now Ikav was a mighty man,
a miner brave and sure.
Six miners set for work that day
for a twelve-hour tour, a twelve-hour tour.

The weather started looking good
and Alfred's cart was tossed
if not for the courage of D crew boys
poor Alfred would be lost, poor Alfred would be lost.

Alfred came in for lunch that day
a salami in his hand,
not certain what to do with it,
he took it in his hand.
With Ikav and the D crew boys,
the leading hand and his pad,
Alfred took one bite at it
and felt he couldn't stand.

Now here is the tale of what the miners did.
They're here for Alfred too.

They'll have to make the best of things
for Alfred it's an upward climb.

Ikav and his sidekick too
will do their very best
to make poor Alfred comfortable
in their miners' nest.
All phones, all lights, a fuel cart at its best
and a single luxury
like the bonehead operators,
it's primitive as can be.

So seeing Alfred off again
this time on the RFDS plane,
we hope he will be back in a day
and never choke again.

Margareta did go meet Alfred when the flying doctors landed that afternoon at Townsville airport. Coming into the RFDS reception, she ran to Alfred. She then broke her silence in speaking English and ran to Alfred, putting her arms around him.

"My luva, luva, whata happeneda."

Alfred was a bit taken aback as he hadn't heard Margareta in all these years speak a word of English.

"Just a nasty piece of salami stuck in my throat, Margareta," replied Alfred. "Nearly choked me. Fortunately with the help of the paramedics, D crew, and a big cough, we got it out, before they nearly had to make preparations to send me home in a body bag."

Margareta broke down in tears once again and gave Alfred another big hug.

Alfred with Margareta was then taken quickly to Townsville hospital in an awaiting ambulance. The translator was left at the airport. She could catch a bus into town for the hours she may have to wait and look around.

Arriving at the hospital, Alfred was quickly whisked in to see an awaiting doctor.

"Alfred, is it? I see you. You have had an unfortunate episode of choking on a piece of salami. Can you open your mouth and go, 'Ahhh'? Tell me if it hurts, or where it hurts?" asked the doctor.

The doctor thought, *My, what a big mouth Alfred has.*

Alfred went "AHH."

Examining the interior of Alfred's mouth, he saw the rawness where Alfred had coughed the lodged salami up.

"Alfred, you are a very fortunate man. Not many people survive a serious case of salami blockages, especially to the throat. One bite into a sandwich and a salami swallow will instigate a chokehold."

"You mean salami is off the menu?" Alfred asked.

"I'm afraid so," said the doctor. "You will be a little sore in the throat for a few days, Alfred, but that's to be expected. Drink lots of water, gargle before you go to bed, that will keep any infection out. You can go back to work if you wish, or take a few days off to rest up. I'll give you a doctor's certificate."

With Margareta here, Alfred knew exactly what he would do with a few days' rest. The casino hotel was not far away.

Alfred hadn't been to Townsville for some time and a treat for Margareta would be just the thing to put Alfred into her good books, if you know what I mean.

In Spain, do what the Spanish do. In Aus, do what the Aussies do, whatever that is.

The two days off, Alfred and Margareta would live it up.

Would there be any other medical issues Alfred would have to sort out before the bobsled championships in Japan?

Worst case scenario, the bobsled team had never seen snow, and Trevor and Roger with the long beards would have to contend with frozen hair on their faces in the extremely low temperatures.

THE TRAINING SESSION

The team had made it to the camp after the day shift swing at the mine had finished. Alfred would fly down and be picked up for the training.

Because there was no ice, everything at this stage would be done on wheels and the crew would be slowly broken into the ice part of the training in Japan a few weeks before the competition.

The team had to qualify time wise before the competition and this is what the company was looking for, as they knew they had an unbeatable product on the line, this being the structure and the fabric of the bobsled. Only Alfred knew at this point why the mining company had taken an invested interest in Alfred's bobsled plan. They wanted to promote under secrecy the world's fastest bobsled ever.

This, Alfred thought, was a safety concern but he wasn't going to break this news to the team yet, as this would cause some panic and possibly a bit of disharmony amongst the team. Alfred had to have a plan. Alfred was thinking about this on the plane to Mackay. You always had to have a plan. Be one step ahead of everyone else.

With the speed this newly-designed bobsled could travel at, an impact of a crash could cause fatalities. This was a new team and these were his friends. They had just helped save his life from the choking incident and he wasn't going to put their own lives in jeopardy. Ikav was the biggest and heaviest, he was positioned down the back. Ikav was the weight equaliser, Trevor Keen was the middle man (and even with a helmet on, he would feel the cold under his hairy beard), Drew was the driver with Steady Ernie behind him, Roger Macfarlane in between, Trevor Keen and Roger Macfarlane and Ikav.

Alfred had an idea; it wouldn't break any rules of a bobsled race and would absorb the serious impact of a crash. The company wasn't interested in the safety of the crew, although Alfred and crew were trying to make it a top priority. "Toilet rolls, yes, toilet rolls."

What made Alfred think of toilet rolls. Well, they had Trevor Keen King of the toilet rolls. Toilet rolls were light and cost effective and can take a punch. That was it, just before a race would start, a big box of toilet rolls would be thrown in between all the team members. This would keep the officials guessing. And if the speeds were phenomenal, the toilet rolls would cushion any impact. Just like the air cushion in a car set off after a crash. That's perfect, Alfred. Keep everyone guessing, even the team.

The flight had landed in Mackay. Alfred had spent an enjoyable two days with Margareta and she had definitely made it worthwhile. Alfred came to the training camp with a smile on his face. He had been picked up in a company Land Cruiser and was taken directly to the camp facilities.

Arriving there midafter, the land cruiser door opened and there was the team to welcome Alfred, their furious leader and designer.

There was a purposely built velodrome, and training facilities, gym, accommodation, kitchen. It was all there. *This has to work*, thought Alfred. *They're either going to approach the speed of sound or the bobsled machine is going to fall apart on high impact.* Either way, Alfred was going to prepare for this under secrecy. The company didn't know what Alfred had planned for. The team were just there for the thrill, whether the team would continue after this as adrenaline junkies or not. They would have accomplished something many Queenslanders would never achieve, race at high speed on ice.

Trevor Keen had given up his smoking habit and saw the benefits of keeping fit. Ikav had lost weight but built strong muscle as many islanders do. He looked great. Drew and Ernie looked in good shape as well from the diets. That left Roger Macfarlane, a quiet reserved fella, picked because he had the incentive to really push himself and maintain his fitness. Most of the crew although dedicated were out for a laugh and that was Alfred's motto.

Life is too short to be serious all the time.
So if you can't laugh at yourself, call me
and I will laugh at you!

The team met together, ate together, trained together, and slept in the same dorms together. Every morning was a 5.30 a.m. start, with breakfast and a briefing given by Alfred and training specialist.

Alfred made sure the trainers were not all female or the team would be concentrating on the trainer and not the training. Good plan, Alfred.

Once the physical training was done, into the bobsled and around the velodrome. Of course the wheels under the bobsled compared to the proper ice skies would give a slightly different effect, but the principle would still be the same and yes, the speed difference when the team really became balanced would be phenomenal. The concern for Alfred was the uncontrollable speed if the team lost control. The only consolation was the abundance of toilet roll padding. *It will work,* thought Alfred.

Management from Nandi mine sent two representatives down to the training camp twice a week over those four weeks. They were ensuring the skin and structure of the bobsled was keeping its integrity under high speeds.

Alfred had cottoned on to this and ensured the tub with the team in it was toilet roll complete. The team thought it was great joke. Well, it was till a close incident happened. Fortunately that day, management representatives were not at the camp.

The speed of the bobsled had reached over 90km/hr when

Drew lost control. The speed was phenomenal. The bobsled rolled. Everyone inside was unharmed. The toilet rolls had absorbed the impact. You could say this was a crash course. Even the toilet roll king, who made the loudest noises, was amazed.

Alfred's plan had worked in an unexpected test roll. The mining representatives were not around to see this, and this was a good thing. Maybe it was time for Alfred to explain to the team what management was really involved in, regarding the sponsorship.

As the team regrouped and brought the bobsled back on its wheels, moving it to the start of the velodrome, Alfred called an urgent meeting.

"Everyone okay?"

Drew and Ernie spoke up.

"Little shook up, but where did you come up with the idea of the toilet rolls, Alfred?"

Then Trevor Keen spoke a few words. "I hope you are not going to raid my cupboard again for toilet rolls."

Every one of the team laughed.

"Listen up," said Alfred. "Got something really important to tell you and I hope this doesn't scare you off."

Everyone's faces dropped a bit.

"The reason management have sent representatives from the mine to observe is that the fabrication and structure of the bobsled you are all riding in has been built from hi-tech light and strong alloy, never been used before in racing. They are expecting you as the team to qualify and reach speeds never achieved before. They don't know that I had found out about this. The toilet rolls will absorb any form of impact and won't increase much weight. You have proved toilet paper works with the crash you have just come through."

"Is every one of you still prepared to go through with the training and the competition? If not, we stop right here," said Alfred.

There was silence for a minute as the team absorbed what Alfred had just said. Ikav and Trevor Keen broke the ice.

"Let's do it."

Then there was a big cheer. There was three weeks before leaving for Japan's bobsled tournament. Every day the team was working as a team. Alfred saw the improvements every day. Even Alfred's strides and alertness seemed to improve also, not to say he wasn't alert before.

The speed obtained on the bobsled was phenomenal. The wheels at 120km/hr were just about falling off. The ice would make the difference, as of no moving parts. If the Jamaican team who had never raced a bobsled on ice before could do it with a rundown old bobsled, this would be a breath of fresh air in becoming the world's fastest bobsled.

Alfred had another idea for the team. He wasn't going to tell them yet, but the team had been awarded individual contracts to sign, by the company. With the information Alfred had, no contract should be signed unless they, the team, could get royalties from the company after the race for every bobsled or machinery sold. The mining company would then know that Alfred, yes Alfred, had found out about their plan. There would be no payouts to keep the secret secret; the mining company would have to go along with Alfred's plan for the time being until they could find some loophole in the individual contracts.

If Alfred's team was successful, it wouldn't matter, at least for a while. Alfred and the team could take the glory and the company could take the money. But the question that would always be asked, how did Alfred find out about this new alloy? And how far was he willing to go with these royalties?

We will soon find out. Alfred too had made future plans and this could all work out in his favour.

Alfred had another problem looking back at the castle. Margareta had arrived back at the castle to find that the greenies had tried to barricade the drawbridge. They were fewer in number as Alfred's water pets had been fed well, but they still were aggressively trying to make a point. Alfred had two options to consider when he got home. Wait for the next few weeks of rain to wash them out or he had plans to keep them on a reservation in on his surrounding boundaries outside the castle moat and drawbridge. We will see what happens when he gets back from Japan.

Margareta would be safe enough with security and her German staff. They really were becoming family and they didn't want to leave. But being young and adventurous, there was more of the world to see. They promised Margareta a time frame, with the intention of coming back after their travelling around. But would they? Time will tell when the world is rapidly changing. They have security at Alfred and Margareta's castle and they have the pet lizards who demolish any predators.

That gave them all peace of mind. And they had good neighbours either side of the castle. A little old and dotter, but like every old person, a wealth of information. Albert Einstein junior and his wife Ingrid on one side, and Thomas Edison junior on the other side. Cannot go wrong with families of scientists and inventors. Even Alfred proved that. Alfred had promise to used Albert Junior's law of relativity in every aspect of his life. Of course it would relate to building projects in Alfred's mind.

There might be validation for the law of relativity required for the bobsled project. Let's see what Alfred has in mind.

It doesn't matter if the glass is half empty or half full...Be grateful that you have a glass and there is something in it.

Alfred thought about those words for a minute. Alfred didn't have a glass, but he knew if he had one, it would be full and he was grateful for that.

Alfred's family and friends gave him that inspiration and drive. Yes, Alfred's ways were a little different to everyone else's. You could call him unique and that's what made him a people person. Alfred got this bobsled team together on an idea. And that idea had been manipulated by the mining company Alfred worked for. But Alfred knew how to turn the tables unwittingly. Alfred was planning for future events, that gave him royalties to build the village and aquatic centre in his castle grounds, not only for him but the benefits from royalties for his bobsled team.

Alfred had promised to share the spoils of the aquatic centre with Ikav and his family for the effort Ikav had put into helping Alfred with the hole and tunnel boring for the pool utilities, as Alfred kept good on his promises.

JAPAN, HERE WE COME

Centuries ago, they would say all roads lead to Rome. In Alfred's case, all bobsleds lead to Tokyo, Japan.

The training had been intense, and to climatise a little in Queensland, Alfred used a chiller so the team would know what sort of winter temperatures they would be expected to race in. Each member, dressed in thermal and winter clothing, would spend up to an hour at a time in the chiller over those four weeks. The initial shock was huge, even with the thermal gear on, but after a few days, even Alfred could handle it. No one on the team suffered frost bite, that was a good thing.

Margareta was so impressed, she had asked Alfred if she could meet Alfred and the team in Tokyo. She was a team supporter and there would be many. Half of D crew had decided to take their holidays at the same time. Or if they were not allowed to, they went on sick leave. This was something they weren't going to miss. To them, especially with Trevor Keen and Ikav racing, it was something they themselves couldn't take seriously as Trevor was not a serious person and Ikav was a gentle giant. How wrong they would be. In four weeks after Alfred's briefing, the team had taken this opportunity very seriously. They knew what was at stake and the potential for their futures with the royalties promised over a period of time in the mining company contract.

The team had reached nearly 150km/hr and had stayed upright on wheels following the first accident. This was something never dreamed of, as when you saw the first pictures of Alfred's primitive idea in the Heavy Vehicle workshop on site nearly a year and a half ago.

Bert Munroe, the New Zealander, was never taken seriously

either when he turned up with a 1923 modified Indian motorcycle on the salt flats racing track in Utah USA, especially when he had cut the tread off the tyres. When the officials reluctantly let him race as the backing from other computers, Bert Munroe broke the world record at Bonneville in 1967 at the age of sixty-eight. The modified 1923 Indian Scout reached 296km/hr for a motorcycle under 1000cc. That record still stands in 2020.

Alfred had read up on Bert and was fascinated by the ingenuity of his fellow Kiwi brother. He had worked on some of Bert's principles with speed modifications and safety. Although Bert had been dead for a number of years, his legend still lives on as the World's Fastest Indian.

Could it be Alfred was preparing the team as the World's Fastest Bobsled?

Let's see what Alfred names the bobsled and this will give us some idea of his thinking.

Alfred's crypto currency had dropped significantly so, having precious metals now as a backup and the royalties written into the mining bobsled contract, Alfred and Margareta and the team should come out okay. Alfred was still on track with his retirement plans. It was looking like Alfred was now in the planning of building his own kingdom and own network. Let's see what happens once again when Alfred eventually returns home.

The day had come to board the Qantas A330 for Tokyo, Narita airport from Brisbane, Australia. A little nervous, not knowing what lay before them and Alfred as their leader, this was an achievement. The team knew it. They had built from scratch a blueprinted bobsled, they had trained from scratch, physically, emotionally, and mentally, they had had the support from families, friends, and of course D crew. The mining company had paid all expenses, allowances and living costs, as they knew this would pay off big time for them. The world was going to be taken by surprise, by an unprofessional bobsled team that would soon become a professional bobsled team. They were a team of miners from deep in the heart of North West Queensland, Australia who were going to take on the world's best.

The team's logo was Nandi United. And the packed and ready bobsled was none other than "the World's Fastest Miners." Painted in Nandi company colours, blue and orange.

Alfred, you really excelled yourself again. Alfred had made sure of the abundance of toilet rolls, packed both inside and outside the bobsled. The bobsled itself was being contained and freighted to Narita, Japan separately.

Before leaving the Qantas lounge that day. Qantas had made provisions for the team. Nandi mining company management had been there congratulating the team on their efforts and wishing them every success. Alfred got up and made a few necessary comments.

"I would like to thank you all personally, you shared the dream and here we are," said Alfred. "Most of you were at the pool party and the fun time we had there as you all made that happen as well. We will have some fun and make this happen again on the world stage. Every one, just remember to stay hydrated with water, you can have your fun after the competition. Enjoy yourselves and remember, I have to get you all home in one piece, so remember to stay and work as a team.

There was some clapping and cheering in the lounge from team, management, and Qantas staff.

"One last thing, a reminder, the Australian and New Zealand national anthems will be played and represent our countries."

"Who's the kiwi?" called out Trevor Keen.

"I'll let you find that one out for yourself, Trevor," replied Alfred.

And with that came the call over the lounge PA that QF509 to Sydney was boarding at Gate 22.

The Qantas flight would take them to Sydney and the team would depart Sydney for Singapore on QF81 and then Narita, Japan.

Alfred had known the dangers of the killer speeds this machine could handle and had prepared every safety measure to keep his team safe on the ice velodrome. These measures had not been implemented in company policy as it was not a mining operation. But Alfred would make sure every member of his team would get home safely.Everyone would have to do a take five and before any timed race, the team together would have a sit down and do a JSA (Job Safety Analysis) which included the hazards, the risks, and the measures to counteract those risks. For Alfred, this was still a mining operation on an international scale, but on ice and not on a coal pit.

Boarding the A330 and being acknowledged by the Qantas cabin crew, the captain made a special announcement as making the team very welcome. The team Drew Berryman, Ernie Cripps, Trevor Keen, Ikav AMI, Roger Macfarlane, and Alfred Chuck Norris. But who was the mystery Kiwi (New Zealander) Alfred had talked about? The answer would come when Margareta and the D crew supporters would meet up in Tokyo for the world champs.

By the way, the mining team had broken Australian records in a short space of time. No one knew anything about this rookie crew, but Australia was soon going to find out what this mining team was all about.

The flight from Brisbane to Sydney was a short one hour thirty-five minutes, with a three hour stopover at Sydney airport, then another eight hours twenty minutes to Singapore with stopover, and another seven hours ten minutes from Singapore to Narita, Tokyo.

Every one of the team was tired on arrival, but the good thing about it, the mining company had booked and made all the arrangements for Alfred and the team and the training venue available before the championship meet. The bobsled had already landed at Narita ahead of the team and would be on its way to the training venue.

"Everyone, listen up," called Alfred. "We may all be a little tired, but I can assure you, this is something we are not going to miss. I have been informed that there is curiosity going around the teams competing, who are the new rookies. We are not going to give them the satisfaction of anything. We are to be friendly, courteous, and focussed. We have reached phenomenal speeds in training and the competitors don't even know we have broken the world record speed of 205 km/hr and all they know is the name, 'The World's Fastest Miners,' this being an entry to the competition and the speed for qualifying."

This has given them some laughs.

"That's okay," said Alfred. "Tomorrow, we start. I suggest we all get a good night's sleep and start fresh at five o'clock in the morning."

Wow, that was a real mouthful, Alfred. From humble beginnings to racing with the best, Alfred, you have really made your mark. If you pull this off with your team, the sky is the limit.

That afternoon Margareta arrived with some of the team supporters from D crew. The others would follow on a later flight. Also with Margareta was the mystery Kiwi bloke. He wouldn't show his face to the team till the team was well under way in the competition.

Margareta and Alfred now would make a good combination. Margareta was getting over her English barrier and refusal to learn English due to past English and Spanish history, sounding out a few more English words. Margareta would also become the mother of the team. Yes, she would have input.

The supporters would stay at a hotel nearby, as the team had strict instructions from mining management to stay and play together. That was their only stipulation.

Trevor Keen and Drew were becoming a bit restless that night and kept everyone awake for a few hours with their crazy talk. The talk would eventually send them to sleep, but not without some very ropable team members in the morning at the 5 a.m. start.

The bus drove the team to the training facilities. There were other teams from around the world setting up to commence their training. When they saw this new team pull up and set up their shining new bobsled that had aerodynamic wings on, there was a great laugh.

"I think you boys have come to the wrong tournament. The flying competition is not too far from here and they are practicing with their aerobatics," someone called out.

There was a great laugh.

"Everyone, keep your cool," said Alfred. "They don't know what we know. Stay focussed, team. They are really going to laugh when we set those boxes of toilet rolls in motion, and it won't be a bowel motion either," said Alfred.

The team laughed.

"Remember, everyone, stay focussed."

There was another sling off.

"Hope you boys don't roll over on the ice going too fast."

Another round of laughs.

That was really an understatement and Alfred thought, *He who laughs last has the last laugh.* Hmm how true, Alfred. Where does Alfred get all his information from, one has to ask.

The team had prepped up. All their gear was on. Alfred had enrolled the team under the "World's Fastest Miners" and that name alone was beginning to get some interest.

The team's slot to roll down the ice velodrome was number fifteen. The highest speed so far was recorded from a German bobsled team of 180km/hr, followed closely by an American team of 179/hr. Most teams at their best were reaching just over 170km/hr.

There were two more competitors, one from Canada and another from Czech Republic, before the "World's Fastest Miners" would be let loose.

The Canadian team went through and clocked up 175km/hr on the first-time trials. The Czech Republic team never made it the end right way up as they crashed and slid to the end. They had two more chances to qualify.

It was now the "World's Fastest Miners" turn to roll up.

"Remember, Drew, Ernie, Trevor, Roger, and Ikav, stay focussed," Alfred whispered, and then dumped three boxes of toilet rolls between all the seats.

There was a great roar of laughter.

"Team Miners, are you going to take out a latrine and the end of the velodrome?"

Then more laughter.

The overhead clock was counting down. The team were ready to start the run up. Three, two, one.

The race was on. Drew jumped in first then Ernie, followed by Trevor and Roger and, last but not least, Ikav. Those strong flaring muscles of Ikav were the last to push the miners' bobsled into fast motion before Ikav jumped in.

The aerodynamic wings were stabilisers as the team knew now their final speed would reach over 200km/hr.

The speed began to pick up as the miners' sled went around the first bend. The bobsled was a bit wobbly as they rounded the bend. Working together the speed was gaining momentum. 150km/hr at a quarter of the tunnel, then 160km. Approaching halfway 175km/hr then 180/hr/ then 190km/hr. Nearing the finishing line, they had reached over 205km/hr. The braking system was working hard as they slowed down after crossing the finish line.

"205KM/HR. My, that is astonishing for a first-time competitor," called the commentator.

He had been following the miners' machine with great interest and excitement as the speed increased over 170km/hr.

As the bobsled was hauled back up to the training area, Alfred, in strident pace without slipping in the snow, yes, Alfred too had never seen snow before, met his team.

"Team, that was a good start," said Alfred. "We cannot become complacent; we have to continually think as a team."

The commentator wanted to get hold of the miners' team manager but Alfred was nowhere to be seen.

As the team made it back to the training area, they were confronted by the Germans, Americans, and Canadians.

"How did you manage to pull that off, Miners? You must have found some way of cheating," said the German captain with a strong accent. "We want an investigation into your bobsled by the competition's official."

There was no jeering or small talk now. Just a bitter feeling of rookies outwitting professional teams.

The team miners went back to their venue where Alfred and Margareta were waiting for them.

Drew, Ernie, Trevor, and Roger high fived. But Ikav had a frown on his face.

"What's up, Ikav?" Alfred asked.

"As soon as I went running and being the last man in the bobsled, as I jumped in, the back end of my team uniform split right up the middle. I had to sit there when we stopped and wave someone down for a towel to cover up."

There was a roar of laughter, this from the home team.

"It's okay, we brought extra-large sizes," said Alfred, trying to contain himself.

Then Ikav let out a great burst of laughter with all the other team members.

"Everyone, once again great effort. You will now have some very jealous and confrontational competitors. But that's okay," said Alfred. "Our main goal is not to just win, but show the world we can build anything light and strong with this material only formulated from this company. Our royalties depend on it."

There were another four races in the completion and it would look like the "World's Fastest Miners" would be leading the charge in the next round.

The complaint made to the officials was now official and the miners' bobsled would be scrutinised for anything that would cause the team to cheat. There was nothing in the racing code that could disqualify a team from having toilet rolls added either. But it would be interesting if they could interview Alfred and ask why.

Alfred was the representative of the team and he was happy to show the officials around the miners' bobsled. There were a few visiting cameras as well.

The inspector looked inside, outside, underneath, and then tried to push on it.

"Alfred, this is very light, isn't it?"

"It doesn't break any weight problem rules, does it?" Alfred asked.

"No," said the officials.

"The structure is in the form of a bobsled?" Alfred asked.

"Yes," said the official.

"And is there any speed enhancer?" asked Alfred.

"No," replied the official.

"So what's the problem?" asked Alfred.

"We had a complaint, and we have an obligation to investigate to make every competitor compete ethically. By the way, why all the toilet rolls? Is this an Aussie thing?"

"In good time, you will find out," said Alfred. "Is there anything else I can help you with?"

"As a matter of fact, there is," said the official. "We would like to interview you and the team and let the public know a little about the team's background."

"In good time," said Alfred.

Alfred was playing it down, a man of few words. He and the team had to stay focused. There was nothing stopping the team reaching those same speeds as they had done on the training course in Queensland, the only difference being on ice not rollers.

Alfred gave the team a final briefing before some leisure and chow time. They had an early night for the early start the following day, 5 a.m.

Margareta made sure every team member was happy before they turned out the lights. Yes, everyone was happy for day one.

The D crew supporters had turned up for the following day's elimination. They had heard there was a rocket machine in front and knew it could only be the "World's Fastest Miners" machine. They would be there early to support their team and also the mystery Kiwi.

It's gonna be a very short time
till the icing racing brings them round again to find.
Alfred, they thought, would always be at home
Oh, no, no, no.
He's the ice rocket man
and setting up the ice machine there alone again.
Alfred the rocket man.

Yes, it takes a certain person to build or have the inclination to build a rocket on ice and yes, we can call Alfred the "ice rocket man."

Day two of the competition, the miners had the fastest time and fastest speed. In the preliminary, the fastest miners were looked down on as being rookies, then they were suspected of cheating. Now the competition's on. "The World's Fastest Miners" were up first. Could they beat their record first run?

Once again, Alfred had given them their pep talk, fired in three boxes of toilet rolls in between every team member. This time no one laughed, there was an intrigue as no one knew exactly what the toilet rolls were for.

The team held the fastest speed and time. If no team matched them and for some reason they rolled, they would still make it to the semifinals.

The clock was ticking down, the team was ready to run and jump in. Four, Three, Two, One, Go.

Drew and Ernie jumped in first, then Trevor and Roger. Then, pacing fast, the big man jumped in. This time his pants didn't split. What happened next nearly put the team out of the whole competition.

Taking the second bend, Drew lost control and the bobsled flipped. The impact upside down didn't compress the bobsled but the toilet roll, compacted between the riders, compressed the impact, saving the team from serious injury. Drew broke his arm, smashing against the side structure.

There was some nervousness from officials and spectators as the bobsled had not made it out of the tunnel. Alfred and some emergency service personnel quickly moved down the bobsled lane. They found the miners' team upside down, seemingly lifeless. Then the voice.

"Is everyone still alive?" called out Trevor Keen.

"Drew's broken his arm," called Ernie.

"Roger, Ikav, you both complete?"

"All good here," called Ikav.

Just as the team were trying to get out, help arrived.

"Is everyone okay?" called the paramedic.

"We are all good," called Trevor, "just one suspected broken arm."

Alfred came down the tunnel as well.

"Everyone okay! Everyone okay?" Alfred called out.

The team was a little shaken but, except for Drew, all were okay. Drew had smashed his right arm against the dash, but the compacted toilet rolls had cushioned any sort of impact for the rest of the team. Alfred's idea worked again.

"Drew has broken his arm but the rest of us are okay," called out Trevor, as the team were being helped.

"Well, I guess this is it," said Ikav. "We don't have a driver."

"Not so fast," said Alfred. "We'll get Drew the medical attention he needs and then everyone to our meeting room."

None of the other teams had cleared 200km/hr and it was frustrating them. They knew now the only chance of victory was if the World's Fastest mining team were out of the competition by default not disqualification. They had no driver or so they thought.

However, the mystery driver that had come with Margareta, yes, the Kiwi, was about to be revealed by Alfred when everyone on the team was together.

A little cold and a little shaken, the mining team met in the conference room allocated to them.

Alfred spoke first.

"Team, we are still in the competition which the other teams are going to hate," said Alfred. "Remember our mystery Kiwi from NZ. Well, here's Leigh Roy Brown. I'm sure most of you know him."

"Leigh Roy!" said Trevor with mouth wide open and followed with Ernie, Roger and Ikav scratching their heads.

"Leigh Roy has been training just as hard as you fellas," Alfred said. "As a matter of fact, he has been watching you train and simulated bobsled racing as driver. Team Miners, your new driver."

Ikav had a few words to say.

"Leigh Roy, I hope you are not going to drive the sled like you drive a plane."

"Don't worry, Ikav, it will be great," replied Leigh Roy with a smile on his face.

Yes, Leigh Roy was back. And the mining team was back in the competition.

The other international teams followed on after the Miners' sled crashed. The Germans first, their top speed 190km/hr crossing the finish line, then the USA team reaching tops of 185km/hr and the new challengers, the hosting team Japan at top speed of 187km/hr. This was a little frustrating, maybe more than a little frustrating as a new rookie team from Queensland, Australia, where there is no snow, had taken a lead position and had never raced before. How was this possible with all these very experienced bobsled teams? The Miners' team had crashed, had not burned, still had the fastest time and speed over two races and were now in the semifinals.

There was a day stand down before the semifinals. The Miners' bobsled was kept away from the public eye until the competition was over. Prying eyes and prying cameras were not on Alfred's agenda. And this too would keep other teams speculating.

The Miners' team still held the fastest speed, time and, in Leigh Roy's mind, there was still some more speed to come. He wasn't going to make mention of that but by the twinkle in his eyes, Alfred knew something was up.

The day of rest had given the Miners' team not only a reprieve but freshness, having rested up for the semifinals twenty-four hours later. The team with their new driver Leigh Roy were in for a ride of their life.

Lining up under the digital clock above them, the countdown began. The team were rocking backwards and forwards, ready to jump in the sled. Five, four, three, two, one. After the countdown, they were off. Leigh Roy jumped in first, followed by Ernie, Trevor, then Roger and finally the big man with all his might, Ikav. This time, his track pants didn't split. They were off to another good start. Leigh Roy took the steering phenomenally well. The speed steadily rose to 90km/hr then 120km/hr, then soared to a speed of 190km/hr then 205km/hr, closing the finish line at a whopping

215km/hr. Slowing the sled down was the next biggest hurdle and it did come to a standstill after a few hundred meters.

A jubilant Alfred and supporters from D crew were there to meet the team. There were also interested reporters and excited public viewers.

The team motto was:

We are the boys from down on the mine.
We really know our sled.
There's much better in value in Nandi.
We travel at high speed.
Our sled slices thinly. There's no stopping
and boy, she moves at super pace.
Nandi mining, much better
than ever.

There was a roar from the crowd, as they began to understand a little of the unknown about this bobsled team. They were from Australia and they were all miners of some sort.

But what was the purpose of racing in this tournament? That was the question being asked by everyone. If it wasn't for winning, what else?

The challenges from Germany, USA, Japan, Poland, France, and Belgium knew there was something in the structure and fabrication of that bobsled that made it so unique and they were all itching to find a sample of the Miners' bobsled. The Miners were rookies, not professionals like them, so they thought.

Alfred kept everything as securely tight as possible. If there was any sabotage to the sled, Alfred always had a plan B, just like the plan B he had for a backup driver. Smart move Alfred.

But wait and see what happens in the two days remaining before the finals.

In the meantime, Alfred and Margareta had decided to take the team for a night on the town, in downtown Tokyo. No, there were no SUKI bars to hang out in or ladies of the night to hang around. This was a team stay together night with entertainment way better.

They had sushi and seafood. Ikav's dream was to wrestle a sumo wrestler. The opportunity did come however as the team walked into a sumo match. A promotion for anyone to take on a sumo wrestler for a prize. Well, most people don't or wouldn't take on a 150kg, what looked like an obese man in a ring and either get thrown out or pushed out without any effort from the sumo wrestler, but when it came to Ikav, he liked a challenge. Ikav was only 120kg and physically strong, you could say close enough but not quite close enough in weight.

When the challenge came up in the ring, Ikav was the first up. He ripped off his shirt and trousers then stripped down to his budgie smugglers. The official, then announcing the challenger to face his champion with a smile on his face, called to let the entertainment begin. The two men bowed as this was custom, squatted then ran to make contact. It was first to push, shove, or squeeze the other out of the circle. The crowd roared. Ikav's D crew supporters, along with Alfred and the team, roared.

"Ikav! Ikav! Ikav!"

It was a daring effort by Ikav to challenge this professional overgrown man called the sumo, but with all his strength it wasn't enough to push the sumo wrestler out of the ring. Within a minute Ikav was pushed out of the circle. It was a great effort and the applause would follow for Ikav. Even the sumo, with a smile on his face, bowed before the two men left the circle.

Alfred, holding Ikav's clothes was signalling to the team and the D crew supporters that tables in a nearby seaford restaurant had been arranged for the meal that night.

One person though was missing. There was no sign of Leigh Roy. Everyone was supposed to stay as a unit but Leigh Roy had gone (in the Aboriginal term) walkabout in a city of so many million people.

Alfred had a hunch where Leigh Roy was. Fast cars, fast machines, fast and furious. There were go-carts racing a block away. This would be the most central path to look for Leigh Roy, leaving Margareta to mother the team and the D crew supporters till Alfred returned with Leigh Roy.

Alfred quickly walked down to the first block where the go-cart racing was being held and, within minutes found Leigh Roy trying out one of those go-carts at high speed in a roped off area.

Waiting for Leigh Roy to finish his three laps, Alfred stood there with a frown on his face in front of the spectators' platform, waving Leigh Roy down.

Seeing Alfred with a concerned look and knowing Alfred would give a complete dressing down on why he, Leigh Roy, should take more responsibility as a team member would make him think more about his actions. For every action there is a reaction. This is the law of the universe.

When Leigh Roy did pull over in the go-cart, Alfred confronted him.

"Leigh Roy, if you had crashed and burned, this could have jeopardised all the team's hard work," said Alfred. "We have already got Drew with a broken wing and besides, we owe this to the mining company who have set us up and negotiated all our contracts with positive results, if we win the speed race in the bobsled."

Having fun was one thing, but taking it to the extreme at the expense of the team was something else. Leigh Roy may have landed a plane in an emergency with his skills of flying, having flown on a commercial licence, but he wasn't experienced enough to suffer a high-speed crash in a bobsled, especially one with this design as being light and fast. Alfred knew Leigh Roy was an adrenaline junky and would be implementing some protective safety measures. Let's see what Alfred does.

Alfred also had the Nandi mining company complete a second bobsled that apparently not many knew about, as a backup. This was just in case there was any sabotage done to the existing bobsled, as it seemed to be way out of the league of all those teams competing. Obviously, the other disgruntled teams would make sure their tracks were covered and no discrimination administered if this was the case.

Above all this, Alfred wanted to get Leigh Roy back to join the team and D crew supporters for the meal ordered at the seafood restaurant, downtown Tokyo. Tokyo being a twenty-four-hour city.

The rest of the team with Margareta and the D crew supporters were sitting down eating when Alfred and Leigh Roy walked in. A big cheer as everyone was in celebration mode, with no bias to any of the team members. They were a team that stayed together and supported each other as a team, no matter what.

Alfred made one announcement when ordering.

"No puffer fish, everyone. We don't want to lose any more team members."

Everyone laughed.

The food that night was great. The Japanese chefs came out to the tables, flipping their fish dishes under a fiery flame in the air and then flipping the prepared fish dishes onto each and every one of the teams' and D crew supporters' plates.

Alfred had never seen this done before and, remembering what the salami had caused weeks previously in the crib hut that lunch time, ducked for cover. He didn't feel he was under attack by a slab of fish, but was just taking precautions. Margareta got a little upset as she had double portions of fish landing on her plate. And in her fiery response, she grabbed Alfred and told him off.

Everyone once again couldn't contain their laughter.

After the meal and a few glasses of saki that were inadvertently added, a happy team and supporters made one last excursion, a quick private tour around the city of Tokyo by night in a forty-seater bus. Before the team would leave after the final competition, Alfred had arranged a biking tour for a day trip out of Tokyo. This would be interesting, but let's just see the finishing of the bobsled competition.

That night, arriving back from Tokyo's finest entertainment, everyone including Alfred slept well.

It would be a 5 a.m. start for the team, but now feeling refresh-ed from the night before, Alfred would once again go over the final stages of the bobsled and team events.

But not everyone was happy. The Mining team had been spied on by other teams and management. This was money to them and losing an international competition meant losing sponsorship from big multinational companies.

The speeds reached by the Miners' machine could be made by definition of non-compliance. There had to be a safety breach somewhere. But what these teams didn't know was Alfred as a patriot had a team policy and had enforced this right from the start, exactly how he would have done it in a pre-start meeting or prior to completing his mobile and fuel runs on the mine site.

You got it. "Everyone has to do a take five. And because of high risk involved, everyone before a race had to be involved in writing out a job safety analysis. In this case, a bobsled racing safety analysis."

Smart move, Alfred, this is well thought out.

And so it was, with the brilliance of a safety share, take fives and job safety analysis, this would prepare the team for what was to come.

That night whilst Alfred, the team and the D crew supporters were enjoying themselves, there was a planned break in to the Miners' bobsled consortium. It was carefully planned so that there would be no comeback on any of the other international teams. It was payback time and no one would have been any the wiser.

The bolts were loosened under the bobsled skids at all points, just enough to rattle loose and come off at very high speeds for an inspecting team. Even in an inspection of the bobsled by the team prior to racing, it would never have been picked up. The intruder quietly left the premises, covering his tracks, everything was done, there would be no more Miners' racing team after tomorrow's finals, or so the others teams thought and they could get on with their international professional bobsled racing.

This was a very dangerous and costly move as this could be a killer race for the unsuspecting mining team, not only for demolishing a bobsled but a life-threatening event for Alfred's team.

Wait a minute, Alfred had carefully thought this through. Alfred knew there would be some disgruntled opposition and he explained this to his team, enforcing the hazards on the job safety analysis and the preventions.

Alfred had secretly brought in another bobsled made of the same composition, same handling, and no changes. The only difference was the colour. The name, the World's Fastest Miners, hadn't changed. It had been approved prior by officials without the name on it initially.

That morning Alfred commended the team, went over the plan for the race and reminded Leigh Roy that this was the final race and no stunts. Leigh Roy, with a twinkle in his eye nodded. Alfred knew what that meant and was going to take into account another precaution over and after the finish line.

"Team, we have the second bobsled here." Alfred unwrapped the cover.

"Why a second one?" called Trevor with Ikav looking a little bemused.

And then Roger spoke up for the first time.

"Alfred's been thinking what we should have all been thinking, referring back to the job safety analysis. There is a possibility our bobsled has been tampered with. An official who passed this very room last night has reported some unusual activity," said Roger.

"How do you know that?" asked Ernie.

"As I overheard a conversation from an official talking with Alfred just a few hours ago."

There was now a look of concern on Ernie, Trevor, and Ikav's faces, but not Leigh Roy's. Leigh Roy looked quite calm. This would be the moment of truth.

"Team, here's the plan," said Alfred. "We are racing in the next hour, there are going to be a few very stunned people as we move this bobsled across the starting line. Nandi officials have been watching and have been in constant communication with myself and another company representative in the background. This is it, team, the final race, we are not out to prove a point. We are here primarily to let the world know we hold the royalties to the fastest bobsled in the world, made locally, with local patented materials and we are a team of miners who have trained and stayed together for the duration," reminded Alfred.

There sounded like some professional pep talk in that speech, Alfred.

There were cameras and journalists who still could not get an interview with Alfred and the team before waiting for the final countdown. And yes, there were the Chinese cameraman spies trying their best to find out why this bobsled was so fast, what the composition of the bobsled material was made of so they could take back to China and manufacture something similar. But the most agitated teams now were those that had put their reputation on the line, having found out that their little plan of sabotage had not worked as the Miners racing team had a second bobsled. The wind had been blown out of their sails, so to speak.

The World's Fastest Miners would now take the tournament to a higher level.

Let's see how high they will take it.

The Mining team had lined up their bobsled on the starting line. There were a few minutes before start so Alfred broke them out in the team song:

We are the boys from down on the mine.
We really know our sled.
There's much better value in Nandi.
We travel at high speed.
Our sled slices thinly. There's no stopping.
And boy, she moves at a super pace.
Nandi mining, much better

than ever.

There was a roar from the crowd, as Alfred had secured all the toilet rolls, stepped back and the team took their positions.

The clock was counting down as the team were gently rocking the sled back and forth. Five, four, three, two, one. They were off, running hard. Leigh Roy in first, Ernie and Trevor next, followed by Roger and then the muscle of the big man Ikav, last man in. The tragedy struck, there was a massive big split in Ikav's track pants. He would have to endure a few minutes of temperatures of minus ten degrees. Hopefully he wouldn't get a case of frost bite on his bum. That would not look good for the team photo after the race. Ikav made a real calm effort not to show any anxiety, which kept the team moral up.

Leigh Roy steered this new machine remarkably well as the speed was increasing average the first two bends at 85km/hr, then ramping it up to 150km/hr, then 190km/hr, then 210km/hr then 220km/hr, it was as though Leigh Roy was not going to slow down. The Miners' bobsled had already won the competition to the disgust of other competing international teams, but Leigh Roy wanted to see how fast this machine could go without rolling or breaking up. Just as well, as the toilet rolls were in place for extra padding.

When the speed encroached 230km/hr, the team was getting a little worried.

Ernie yelled out, "Where we going, Leigh Roy? Are we going to slow down?"

Leigh Roy yelled back, "Downtown Tokyo, here we come."

The rest of the team were in a slight state of shock. They were thinking, *Leigh Roy's putting our lives on the line again, we must stop.*

Meanwhile Alfred had contemplated what Leigh Roy's move would be and down from the finish line, he and some of the D crew supporters had installed a safety net, which was strong enough to absorb the impact of the fast-moving bobsled without injuring anyone. Alfred had seen this done before and knew it would work.

His promise was to get everyone home safely and that he would.

The crowds waiting near the finish line behind the barriers were seeing and going to see a bobsled cross the finish line at an unbelievable speed and that it did. Just like a bullet rounding the last bend and across the line. But then the sled never slowed down. It would only be Alfred's safety net that would bring the bobsled to a standstill, a hundred meters after crossing the finishing line.

Like a punch, the bobsled came to a holt. The toilet rolls had taken the impact once again like a cushion.

Trevor was about to get out and punch Leigh Roy for being so reckless, putting everyone else's lives on the line, when he saw Alfred and the cameras rolling. This wouldn't be a good look and he decided to deal with the matter later.

The crowds were swarming around the Miners' bobsled. At least now they could get a close-up view.

Alfred was being pushed for a statement and an interview. It was company policy not to disclose anything relevant about the company and the Miners' bobsled was under protection from any foreign government seeking to know the secret composition of this machine. The Chinese now had been really sniffing hard to find this for the building of their war and industrial complex.

Alfred's comment: "From a dream and humble beginnings... With a team, training, and perseverance, nothing can stop the human spirit from achieving, not even suppression or manipulation."

Alfred, that's a true statement if ever I heard one.

There was a congratulations from Nandi management as Alfred knew he had put the team on the world stage. It wasn't the bobsled itself; it was the composition of the bobsled that was highly sensitive and could be used for industrial equipment. It was an industrial breakthrough.

All Alfred wanted to do now was go home with Margareta and

the team. Alfred had done his tour of duty. He had met the company and team's obligations, for setting himself, Margareta and the team for royalties for families on going.

All Trevor wanted to do was punch Leigh Roy for his recklessness. Eventually Trevor calmed down, no one was hurt, but there was a lesson to be learnt and Leigh Roy needed to learn it. You cannot go on an adrenaline rush forever. Yes, Leigh Roy had saved the day as a second drive and the team was thankful for that.

The initiative of Alfred's toilet paper collection would be broadcast all over the world as an unusual way of damage control.

The transition from the bobsled to the company management was done very quickly. There were people with cameras and any one of them could have been an industrial spy.

Nandi mining company did give a press release, very brief.

"We are very proud of our team and the effort they placed in making it a priority to getting to this competition," a management official called out.

"But what is the secret to the swiftness of this bobsled, considering the weight of the team?" another called out.

"Press conference shortly," called the Nandi official.

Alfred knew management would not give much away and this would be to the disappointment to competing teams. Alfred also knew this was the first and last race his team would race unless they wanted to pursue another competition without him and Margareta.

The chanting kept coming,

"Alfred! Alfred! Alfred!"

The chants got louder and then the Miners' team picked up Alfred and carried him on their shoulders. With a big smile Alfred threw one of his arms up in the air as the crowd roared.

When the celebrations calmed down and the team with Alfred, Margareta and supporters finally left to go back to their hotel. The bobsled was packaged up, but there would be one more failed attempt to scrape a clipping off the bobsled. A Chinese bloke, calling himself a spectator, wanted to get a good photo of the bobsled closeup with a scraper in his hand!

"YER right."

That would be the last seen of Alfred's mining bobsled internationally. The bobsleds would be this time on the same flight home with Alfred and the Miners team. It would remain as Nandi property and the material structure would be their copyright, not to sell the copyright but to sell the material worldwide under copyright.

For now, Alfred and Margareta would be focusing on the castle as their priority when arriving home and in-between Alfred's work commitments.

Alfred had also had to catch up on running of the fuel cart operations as he felt no one could do a better job than him even if it was a love job, as his royalties would now be his major source of income.

But there was also another problem looming with the greenies. Will talk about this shortly.

The building of the aquatic centre and the tourist stores in the castle grounds were in planning mode. Yes, all this thinking was playing on Alfred's mind.

Alfred had also picked up several messages on his answering machine. There was an important or maybe two important messages from the neighbours. The greenies were sabotaging the power scheme. Alfred needed to get back quick to sort this out. He would lose his neighbours' power connections and his hydro scheme otherwise.

Alfred needed the power generation and the royalties now from the mine sponsorship to build his shopping stalls and aquatic centre in the castle grounds.

Crypto currency had backflipped, his horses were being put out to pasture and he needed some more thoroughbreds to reinstate his runaway streak.

Alfred and Margareta's staff were managing.

Alfred had another idea. Oh no, not another idea. This better be a brilliant idea, but Alfred would need to get back to Nandi mine sooner rather than later.

The team needed to rest and everyone that had participated in the strenuous events needed to rest after a long and vigorous few months of training.

The idea was to get Nandi mining company to give false alarms that they were negotiating a deal with the traditional land owners to mine where the greenies were entrenched. The greenies and the land owners were conspiring between themselves to sabotage any utility access to Alfred's castle and surrounding neighbours. Confusion was Alfred's biggest friend as they, the greenies and the traditional land owners, would be fighting amongst themselves. This would work.

Of course Alfred's main priority was to look after the land and surroundings which the castle was on. The traditional land owners would get a good compromise and the greenies would be put on a fenced reservation where they would be happy to live in tree huts, dress in grass skirts, they would live off the land with no conflict of interests with necessities and running water. It was a win win. With no modes of transport, they could grow and eat their favourite plants they had planted. And Alfred and Margareta would be left alone. The traditional land owners would once again get security for their land and water ways outside the castle.

THE HOMECOMING

"Behind every great man is a woman rolling her eyes"
(Jim Carey)

The team boarded the plane at Narita, Tokyo International within twenty-four hours. Everyone was a little, maybe more than a little, tired. The team had been presented with the medals from the competition after the final race. Ikav now had a new pair of pants. Trevor Keen had sorted out his differences with Leigh Roy, although there was still the urge to smash him one. Ernie and Roger lived to see another day and Alfred and Margareta hugged each other.

A day of remembrance, Alfred thought. Nothing quite like a satisfactory feeling. And now they were on their way home to find a hero's welcome for them all.

Alfred did another great thing. He made sure the original flight the team was supposed to be on was transferred to another chartered flight, so he could sneak the team in without any of the public knowing in Queensland, Australia.

The moment they landed, only friends and family were advised of the flight. Most had not seen their families for over a month. The Miners' team had honoured their contract to Nandi mine and the benefits would flow to each family from there. The celebrations would follow.

Alfred's next move was to ensure the D crew remained together. They had been through mining injuries on site, flying doctor encounters, castle retreat parties and now this whole episode with the bobsled. As they boarded the flight to Australia, they began to sing once again,

We are the boys from down on the mine.
We really know our sled.
There's much better value in Nandi.
We travel at high speed.
Our sled slices thinly, there's no stopping
and boy she moves at a super pace.
Nandi mining, much better
than ever.

The applause that went up by Qantas' crew and associated staff lifted the atmosphere as the team was welcomed on board. It was a chartered flight and had two other sports teams with coaches and managers with them as well.

Alfred had this thought as he sat back in his seat and strapped in:

Learn from the mistakes of others.
You can't live long
enough to make
them all
yourselves.
And with that, the quality of your thinking
determines the quality of your life.

Yes, these are great attributes, Alfred. We need more of these.

As the cabin crew closed the doors, the weight on Alfred's eyes were heavy to the point he fell asleep. Margareta was next him as his head fell on her shoulders and he started snoring. Then out of Alfred's tiredness, he began uttering a few words. Margareta now was contemplating that the use of the English language may be useful and in time now her translator would become redundant.

But what was Alfred singing in his sleep?

He'll be coming down the haul road when he comes.

He'll be coming down the haul road when he comes.
He'll be shooting out those fuel haul lines
to those hungry generators
and the water cannons on those slippery roads.

Yes, Alfred was singing in his sleep and when word got around to Trevor Keen and Ikav and the rest of the team, there came a great quire of unusual noises that picked up on Alfred's subconscious voice and they sang, making up more words as they were singing.

Alfred will be swinging on his bobsled when he comes.
Alfred will be swinging on the bobsled when he comes.
He will kick those jackass riders
coming up against him
and know he has a team right behind.

There was a cheer from all and a slight awakening by Alfred as he briefly opened his eyes and then fell back into his subconscious sleep.

Alfred was living the dream and he was going from strength to strength. It would only be a matter of time now Alfred would be invited onto the board of directors for Nandi mining. He had become a real asset they couldn't afford to lose. But would Alfred accept. We will find out shortly.

The fourteen-hour trip from Narita, Tokyo to Brisbane would eventually settle the whole team and D crew supporters down. You can only run for so long on adrenaline before tiredness sets in. There was only one person on the team that seemed to run on adrenaline all the time. You guessed it, Leigh Roy Brown. What was he up to when everyone fell asleep?

Leigh Roy was planning something on their return to Australia. But he couldn't do this now without Alfred's approval. Leigh Roy had already had one written notice and that didn't come from work either. It came from the tournament, so he had to be very careful to prove he could do this without causing anyone to get hurt or damage to equipment. What was Leigh Roy up to? We will find out after the team is back in Australia with all the congratulations and ceremonies done, after every one of the team and D crew supporters are back with their families.

Speed will be involved, I'm sure, as everything Leigh Roy does involves speed. He cannot help himself.

The Qantas cabin crew had made everyone extremely comfortable and were going out of their way to make sure this was a memorable flight. Who knows, the future fabrication of Boeing and Airbus could be made of the bobsled components. It's not hard to imagine. Alfred's bobsled, a simple design now on the world stage, had many intrigued parties keeping an eye on it. Not the bobsled itself but its components.

Could this be the start of a new area without a think tank?

Alfred himself would be happy to disappear into obscurity, he didn't want to do anymore with this project. This was Nandi mining operations now and their new equipment would be made viable with the light, strong, robust materials for the building of their new earth moving equipment. The team reaped the benefits though. That was all they wanted to do and Alfred helped them do it.

The announcement came from the flight deck as the status of the flight.

"Good morning from the flight deck, Captain John Reinehart speaking. We are approximately one hundred nautical miles to the northeast of Brisbane International and will be shortly commencing our descent. Weather is fine with a light southerly breeze. We hope to have you disembarking within the hour.

"A special thank you to the team miners and their D crew supporters. An exceptional challenge which you have won. Thank you for choosing to fly Qantas, good morning.

"Cabin crew, prepare the aircraft for landing.

"Ladies and gentlemen, we are now preparing the cabin for landing. We ask you to have seats upright, tray tables forward and blinds up, thank you."

The Qantas flight landed early that Friday morning. Families and friends had been notified. Also, Nandi management had the time the flight would be landing.

The media and other watchful eyes had been told the Qantas flight would be landing later and of course the flight schedule had been changed intentionally.

Alfred woke to find everyone rubbing their eyes. The cabin crew had made announcements prior to landing, which the team and supporters had vaguely acknowledged.

"Where am I?" called Alfred, as he had woken from the land of Nod.

In some broken English now, Margareta replied, "You ah back ah in the land of ah USA, my Alfred."

There was a cheer from the team and a little excitement.

"We are home," called out Ikav.

The Airbus taxied off the runway to the awaiting airbridge. It was a cool Brisbane morning just at daybreak. Within minutes, the Airbus had taxied up to the airbridge, locked in the cabin door and then opened for travellers to disembark.

Alfred and Margareta were the first to lead the team off the plane towards a small group of family members and Nandi staff. The small group had been allowed through customs to meet.

The official company logo and uniform team miners were wearing was filmed. Alfred and Margareta led the team to have an official "World's Fastest Miners" team photo in front of family and friends.

The media interviews would be taken in by Nandi management and only they would give answers as they saw fit for answering questions later that day.

What Alfred hadn't told the team and management was that he had intentionally left the proto bobsled, yes, the original trolley he and his work colleagues had set up in the workshop two years earlier as a departing present for industrial spies. There wasn't much to pack. They would be scratching their heads, especially the Chinese as how could such a thing as this go so fast and it was on wheels. And, this was one man, not five heavy men.

Alfred, you're a genius.

Alfred became fully awake now, alert to the surroundings. The families would all go home with their team members having passed through immigration. Immigration had also been notified of the team arriving home and there was a big welcome home sign and a cheer from the immigration officers. They too had watched closely the bobsled competition on the big screen. They called them the rookies from Aus.

Alfred and Margareta would catch an early flight out to Rockhampton, but one strange thing happened before everyone departed that morning. There was a fella running through the terminal where the team had just passed through immigration and security in the main concourse. The police were chasing this fella and coincidently that fella happened to run past Alfred. The fella happened to pass this place at the wrong time. Alfred placed his leg out in front, the fella tripped with whatever he had in his hand, he went flying across the floor and knocked himself out. The airport police catching up couldn't figure out what had happened as there was no obstruction in the immediate vicinity. Even knocking someone over, he wouldn't have knocked himself out. The fella was carrying a small amount of drugs and had been picked up by security when trying to board an aircraft, and airport police were notified.

"Well, everyone," said Alfred. "Time to go home and rest up for a few days. We still have the paperwork to sort out for Nandi mining. That can wait for a week or so. You have done us proud."

On that note, the team and D crew supporters dispersed from the Brisbane international airport Concorde with their families. They all, as team members, would have a story to tell.

It was Trevor Keen, Ikav, and Ernie that passed the last loud comments.

"Don't forget to be on the Tuesday afternoon flight for work, Alfred."

There was a laugh and then the crowd got smaller and smaller until they had all left.

It was a late morning Qantas Link flight back to Rockhampton that Alfred and Margareta were on. There was nothing unusual about the flight. As a matter of fact, the flight was on the approach path over the castle into Rockhampton and for the first time Margareta and Alfred would see the magnificence of the castle looking down from the air into the castle grounds and surroundings.

Blue skies
smiling at Alfred
nothing but blue skies
does Alfred see

Bell birds
singing his song
nothing but bell birds
all day long.

Blue days
could be all gone
nothing but blue skies
is Alfred's song.

Alfred reflected on these words flying home. It wasn't until they were on the approach into Rockhampton airport, flying over his beloved castle, that Alfred and Margareta saw the smoke rising. Not from inside the castle but from outside the castle.

There could only be one thing. The greenies were at it again. They must have heard rumours that a mining lease would wipe out their plot and give access to port infrastructure. These were Alfred's thoughts and he could be wrong.

From blue skies to smoking skies as the Dash 8 was on final approach into Rockhampton airport.

The Dash 8 landed late Friday morning. Alfred and Margareta were awaited by their favourite taxi driver who was on standby to whisk them to the castle. The taxi driver Len had also been briefed by Girt the German tourist.

In a panic, Girt had uttered these words in German:

Tie greenies versuchen uns zu rauchen. Sagen sie Alfred, dass er nach hause kommen muss.

The greenies are trying to smoke us out. Tell Alfred he needs to get home.

The taxi left the airport quick smart. Alfred and Margareta would be home within the hour. On Alfred's mind, he was going to sort these greenies out once and for all. There was no help from the local authorities till things got out of control. This to Alfred was out of control and he and his neighbours were going to fix this. These were Alfred's thought on the way home.

Coming over the last hill to descend onto the road leading to the drawbridge, Alfred could see the situation unfolding.

"What the heck?" Alfred called out.

The greenies must have got just a little upset when there were rumours spreading about Nandi mining company taking a lease out right where the greenies had been entrenched through to the waterway. They had to go as low as smoking the outer perimeters of the castle as well as smoking out Alfred's closest neighbors. The greenies lost the plot with Alfred's hydro power plant and waterways. They had to revert to other drastic tactics, and lighting fires was one of them.

As Alfred and Margareta were being driven to the drawbridge access, which now had been lowered by security, they saw figures running away in the midst of the smoke. The neighbours' brick walls had protected them from unwanted smoke levels as their walls were high.

It was pretty much a dumb thing to do by the greenies, a fire had little to no effect on the castle and surrounding neighbours, the only effect it had was on the environment and wildlife. Smoke inhalation to animals was just as cruel.

Why can't these greenies go home and live a normal life like most people? Alfred thought, *instead of being nuisance people living off the backs of others.* Then Alfred thought again, *these people need to nurtured and helped on to the reservation where they would not have to worry about others' problems and the environment of the outside world. Yes, this was the most peaceful resolution for all.*

Tomorrow he would deal with the hydro problem that had been under threat, see his neighbours, talk to his community of German workers, and keep singing his song "Blue Skies." Yes, life was good.

It had been a full on year so far and the achievements Alfred had made were very significant for all.

A meal had been prepared for Alfred and Margareta as a home welcoming. Yes, in the true sense of the word, Bavarian style, no expense spared, and a little German music to go with it.

Alfred came back to reality. It was the Bavarian atmosphere and the fine food prepared for himself and Margareta that made an enjoyable welcoming home present.

Girt and the young German woman had gone out of their way to prepare a banquet meal for Alfred and Margareta. Also it was two of the girls' farewells (Auf Wiedersehen) as they were on their travels. The reality was they had been locked out and locked down over the last two years from inside Australia and locked out from their own country, Germany, due to the global pandemic. And now with easing of restrictions, it was time to broaden their horizons once again. They had also planned to return at some stage. Replacement fill ins were already being prepared so Margareta would still have the full complement of workers.

Tomorrow would be a new day, a time for reflection before Alfred would contemplate on going back to work. But Alfred, you don't need to go back to work in a hurry. You have earned more money in the last two years, with horses, crypto currency, and now royalties.

But, thought Alfred, *if I don't turn up for fuel truck operations, and mechanical rebuilds, I'm going to miss out on my sunrise and sunset events. My voice is going to suffer and my ukulele is going to have cobwebs on it.* And so it was to be, Alfred was to plan once again and juggle work activities with family and circumstances at home.

There was also something else playing on Alfred's mind.

Leigh Roy Brown had asked Alfred about something he had been planning. Anything with Leigh Roy involved speed. The first instance was taking over the flight controls of the aircraft that day when the pilot fell unconscious and, arriving back at Rockhampton airport, Leigh Roy didn't want land right away. Leigh Roy wanted to do a beat up in front of everyone down the runway. And the second one more recent, taking that bobsled to well over 200km/hr to see how fast it could really travel with everyone in it and, to their annoyance, the team wanted to cross the finish line only.

The only thing left was the area just to the south of the castle that the greenies hadn't explored or didn't know that housed a back road to the castle but also was Alfred's unregistered drag strip.

Alfred had been asked on recent occasions about race meetings to be held here and now Leigh Roy wanted to follow up on this in the next two weeks in his 1969 Holden Monaro GT.

Alfred thought, *How much adrenalin does Leigh Roy have?* Alfred wasn't going to rush this decision. There were more important issues, getting to work safely and home again and stage two of revisiting the planned greenies reservation. Yes, the boundaries had all been marked out clearly. They themselves had barricaded themselves into their own designated area and would come out to annoy everyone in the vicinity when they were least expecting it. Alfred had fixed the hydro problem. They, the greenies, had tried to dam and stop the water turbines from turning to produce the welcomed power for the surrounding neighbours and community.

Now stage two would come into effect. Operation take back. Tenders had already been submitted to Alfred in recent months. Alfred had not rushed this as he knew the finance would need to come from well-earned royalties from the bobsled operation and he had been totally focused on this for the last year and half. Now that was over, he and Margareta could refocus.

A successful contractor would start laying the boundary posts in a 5000 sq meter compound of natural forest on Alfred's property. Then greenies had campaigned to stop removal of any forest, natural bush that was on Alfred's property and boundaries. As a matter of fact, Alfred had no intentions of removing or clearing any wildlife or natural reserve. This would not be complete without the greenies living in their tree huts and grass skirts amongst nature that they had fought so hard for. This one thing that Alfred and neighbours agreed on and gave full support to the greenies. Again it would be a win win and they would have their own boundaries.

With tenders closed and a contract to be signed in days, Alfred would be off to work within those few days.

He would recoup from the jet lag, rest from the long hours and weeks of training, be at peace with his home surroundings and his lovely Margareta at his side, who now was able to speak more broken English than ever. Alfred had a plan.

Hi ho, hi ho, it's off to work I go.
It was not:
I owe, I owe, it's off to work I go.
Life was good, so Alfred thought.

The strategy of building the small community medical shopping stalls and aquatic centre he had promised Ikav to be a part of was the final part of the plan.

They say no man's an island. Well, in Alfred's case, it worked in his favour. He had an island with people in it. Inside the castle grounds, to be exact. I wouldn't be surprised in the future if he traded in his own currency backed by a gold standard.

Let's see what happens from going back to work on the Nandi mine site and where this leads to in Alfred's future. I think he's only going back to the mine site to consolidate his royalty payments and finding out about the results of the projected interest in the materials that would sell worldwide under licence, resulting from the bobsled publicity.

Yes, from humble beginnings to this very day, the stories and maybe even folktales might be passed down to the next generation of the life and times of Alfred Chuck Norris.

Let's just see how the final part of Alfred's journey unfolds.

Within the week Alfred was back on site. In the first pre start meeting he had attended in over a month, Alfred got a standing ovation. To those who had taken sickies to the annoyance of the company as D crew supporters to Japan and the team who were all there that morning, Alfred was asked to give the final briefing on the team's success on pulling off a bobsled tournament as rookies.

Management was also there in this particular start and they too were eager to hear of Alfred and the team's experience, knowing full well that their product was so advanced. It would take years for any real competition and that would be the frustration for many manufacturing companies as it would be to their advantage to have and know the product to produce from it.

No government would be able to sell out on them, which was something unheard of. The patent would be kept right here in Australia.

Part of the contract signed by Alfred and the team was that Alfred and every team member had to remain in their occupations and trades till full world orders and production of alloy components for commercial, military, space programs, and aircraft industry contracts had been signed worldwide. This had been negotiated with Nandi mining prior to Alfred committing his team to the world championships in Japan. In this, Nandi mining was liable to their contract. How good was that. Alfred had thought of everything.

Nandi mining was making good head way into the coal and resources for the short space of time they had been operating. Even when returning to site every team member would be shown the changes made over the last month right down to the pit level. For Alfred he was to be shown where he would be refuelling heavy vehicles and generators as the pads had changed as well.

Alfred still held the record for refuelling heavy vehicles by day and night, rain, hail, or shine.

The sunrises would still be there where the three would rush away after pre start, singing accompanied by Alfred's ukulele, but songs now would vary from Morning Had Broken to The Final Countdown.

It was becoming clear that Alfred would be asked to become the ambassador for Nandi mining, and would allow digital displays on the castle walls with Nandi mining as a feature. He figured this would give the greenies in their tree huts something to be entertained by when they were doing nothing and doing nothing was something they did all day anyway, so what had changed. The flashing of signs, especially at night, would give the greenies an extra bit of colour in their lives.

In fact, Alfred had promised the mayor of Rockhampton entertainment and tourism that he would get. The Civil Aviation Authority had already made use of Alfred's castle as a way point for descending air traffic on the final approach into Rockhampton airport from the north. The night lights of the pool and red danger light on top of the castle was more spectacular at night for landing aircraft as the colours lit up the sky without blinding the pilots.

You could see in Alfred's face he was becoming a bit weary.

Never in the course of Rockhampton history has so much been owed by so few.

Is this Alfred we are talking about or someone else?

There were only two things left now to accomplish the finishing touches on Alfred's goal list.

The boundary post and fences were installed to keep the greenies in and Leigh Roy Brown's proposed land speed record on the drag strip.

Leigh Roy had mounted a jet engine to his go-cart. His objective was to run it down Alfred's drag strip at a top speed of 350km/hr without blowing the tyres and crashing.

Leigh Roy was an employee of Nandi mining. But for how long with his royalty pay outs and inventions in the pipeline? Providing he didn't kill himself in the interim, it remained to be uncertain.

And this was Leigh Roy's new baby.

THE RING OF FIRE

Alfred owed no one anything. He would settle all accounts with Nandi mining, going back to work the following day.

There had been a massive heat wave after the cold few months previously and Alfred's motivation of the fuel cart operations was what kept him going. Also, the thought of the final countdown, the drag race on Alfred's unregistered drag strip to the south of the castle, could be something that could go potentially wrong.

But this particular day, Alfred had flown in the night before for the day shift. On his mind had been the tenders for the fencing fabrication and the commencement of the medieval shops inside the castle grounds as a tourist attraction. These had both been accepted by Alfred. No loans were required as payments would now be in gold-backed currency and to top it off royalties ongoing.

Something this day seemed unusually odd. With the heat wave, there seemed to be an unsteadiness on the ground as though the ground had begun to tear apart.

Alfred had pre-started the fuel cart, nothing unusual about that. There was plenty of fuel in the holding tanks and Alfred began to sing his song:

Blue skies.
Nothing but blue skies, ——
do I see.

As Alfred began driving in the heavy fuel cart, there was a massive big BANG. Alfred had trouble trying to keep the fuel cart straight. The road was pulling him to the right. Seeing other vehicles in the same predicament, the big Cat 796s stop on the hall road, drivers climbing quickly down the emergency ladders, it was then Alfred realised it was an earthquake.

Earthquake, Alfred yelled at himself. *Don't panic!*

Pulling up and jumping out of the fuel cart, Alfred ran as fast as he could across the haul road and up the embankment, watching in horror as the fuel cart disappeared into the ground. There was no radio or phone coverage.

Alfred thought, *You can only work with what you got and that can sometimes be stuff all.*

The operators had been picked up quickly and had somehow raced away for some security.

The tremors didn't stop. More cracks appeared on the haul road.

A site emergency once again had been called and, in the background, Alfred could hear the sirens screaming.

Siting high on the embankment, Alfred thought, *Surely in an emergency roll call, they must know I'm missing? Or haven't they completed the personnel numbers on the list yet?*

Alfred couldn't move due to the tremors. He just would have to wait.

Then Alfred began to sing the rest of his song whilst he was waiting:

Bell birds singing his song
nothing but bell birds all day long.

All of a sudden, an emu went running past. If you don't know what an emu is, it's a member of the ostrich family and there were plenty of them on site with other wild life. The animals could sense what was coming as they were running to higher ground.

Everyone at the maintenance workshop were roll called in the crib room in an emergency call out. Two names were missing on the list: Alfred and Leigh Roy. Both had gone in different directions from each other. Both now without comms, as radios were all down.

Trevor Keen, Ikav, Drew and Ernie were back on site from their short break when all this happened.

"Could anyone survive that initial shock? It was recorded as eight on the Richter scale," called Trevor.

"If anyone one could survive that, Alfred could," called Ikav. "He's a survivor."

"What about Leigh Roy?" called Ernie.

"What about Leigh Roy, he's crazy," replied Ikav. "He will be dreaming something up on the way out."

"We could be here for a while," called Drew, "and that makes all the difference to our friends stuck out there."

Meanwhile, the concerns had grown not only from the maintenance workshop staff but operators that apparently had to flee to high ground.

For Alfred, something very unusual happened. The emu came back. He or she was mesmerised by Alfred's singing. It was Alfred's "Blue Skies" song that had captured the emu's attention.

For Leigh Roy Brown, it was a different story. He was about to rise out of the ashes.

Previously, he had been called to a break down in the pit and felt something strange on the road that day. Who was he to call mine control?

Too late. Comms down. Leigh Roy put his foot down, drove the Toyota twin cab as hard as he could. When the earthquake hit, Leigh Roy catapulted the twin cab way over the embankment and into a drainage pond nearby. It wasn't deep and the twin cab was still running, but there wasn't any wheel traction. He decided to get out and make a run for it but his feet got stuck in a lump of mud and he fell face down in the water. What a sight to see.

Picking himself up, waterlogged, covered in mud, he scrambled to the embankment, unrecognisable. The workshop was about two kilometres away. There were still tremors. But for Leigh Roy, this was something else to cause an adrenaline rush. He hadn't seen the big cracks in the ground that had devoured

Alfred's truck as yet. Leigh Roy had only seen the Cat 796s parked up on the road and one digger looking like it was doing a nose dive. Leigh Roy knew it would be a dumb idea to jump in one of the Cat 796s and drive it back to the workshop when they were parked for an emergency.

He was fit and robust. Leigh Roy pulled himself up, climbed up the embankment and ran in between tremors to the maintenance workshop.

For Alfred, a new friend was poking around. He was still captivated by Alfred's singing and had lost all sense of direction.

What Alfred saw next looked like real fun. The emu lowered him or herself, expecting Alfred to get on board. Alfred, realising he was in for a free ride, climbed aboard. Raising him or herself with Alfred on the back, the emu for some reason took off in the direction of the maintenance workshop, avoiding all holes and open cracks in the road. Alfred by now was hanging onto the feathers of the fast-running emu when he spotted a figure running in the distance at great haste. The emu caught up to the runner. And then the runner turned his head around to see an emu running towards him with an object on its back. Suddenly Leigh Roy, seeing the emu closing in and looking in the other direction, misplaced his footing and went flying over the embankment and rolled over the other side.

Alfred saw all this happen and wondered who the runner was. He would have to come back for him as soon as contact had been made at the maintenance workshop to say he was ok. Alfred hoped the emu would also slow down or he would have to jump off as he neared the workshop.

This all happened in a matter of minutes, from an earthquake, to running away from the fuel cart and then seeing it disappear into the ground, to the strange encounter with a lost and captivated emu. Maybe his singing had some strange connotations that was a call of the wild to neighbouring animals and wild life. *What next?* Alfred thought.

Then the workshop appeared. There was no stopping for the

emu, his or her mind was made up, it would keep on running. Alfred would have to jump off and that he did, landing on a pile of hard coal, feeling a lump of coal bruising his buttocks. This wasn't a call of the wild. This was a call of instant pain short lived. Alfred never did see that emu again but that encounter with the emu gave Alfred some other ideas. Let's see what comes of that.

Meanwhile Leigh Roy had knocked himself out cold tripping and falling over the embankment. Coming to, he was beginning to see double. Leigh Roy maybe concussed. All he could remember was being chased by an emu with an object on its back and Leigh Roy had a headache to go with it.

Alfred had gotten himself back to the workshop. Everyone was in the crib hut as the mine had been closed for safety reasons now. The earthquake had now been felt as far as South Queensland, Australia with the brunt being taken in the coal fields. The cracks in the earth had appeared here.

When Alfred walked into the crib hut, once again the cheering went up.

"Alfred you old son, even a cat of nine lives couldn't outdo you," said Ernie.

"What happened to the fuel cart and how did you get back here?" asked Trevor Keen.

"Long story," said Alfred.

"We got time to listen," said Trevor Keen.

"The earthquake was pulling the fuel truck to one side whilst I was trying to keep straight on the haul road," said Alfred. "When I saw the cat 796s parked up on the haul road with ladders down, I realised it was an earthquake as the ground was shaking. Jumping out of the fuel cart and running to the higher embankment, I watched the ground open up and devour the fuel cart as now there were big cracks forming along the haul road."

"So how did you get back here with all the tremors happening?" asked Ikav.

"My singing," said Alfred.

"What do you mean?" asked Drew.

"You know wildlife have a premonition when something drastic is going to happen and they head for higher ground. This emu got disorientated and was mesmerised by my singing of blue skies, nothing but blue skies. I figured there must be some connection with the animal world and my singing as the emu turned around and lowered itself as though it wanted me jump on and so I did. He or she decided to run straight in the direction of the workshop along the back haul road which seemed higher. The emu was not going to stop so I jumped off and landed on my tail bone on a piece of hard coal. Funny too as the emu was racing someone else was running and he disappeared over the embankment. "Who else is missing?" said Alfred.

"Leigh Roy," said Trevor Keen.

"That must have been Leigh Roy diving for cover," called out Alfred. "He's not far away, we got to go and get him."

"Emergency services are dealing with missing personnel," said Trevor.

"But they need to know Leigh Roy is within meters away," called Alfred.

"Leigh Roy's a big boy and an adrenaline junky, he'll turn up," said Ikav.

Meanwhile Leigh Roy, in his state of concussion, and seeing double, was trying to visualise the workshop in front of him. There were still slight tremors. If he went left, he could walk into another disaster area. If he walked right, he could get to the workshop from down on the lower build pad.

With a headache and semi-vision, Leigh Roy headed right down to the build pad. Leigh Roy could hear emergency alarms going off and the emergency vehicles on standby to move in when the tremors had stopped. *There must be more people missing*, Leigh Roy thought. He was now within meters of the workshop having clambered down to the build pad. What Leigh Roy saw there was broken machinery, machinery that must have been worked on prior to the earthquake. The hill to the workshop was his last run.

Planes trying to land also would be turned back for loss of comms. Leigh Roy was now within meters from the crib room, stumbling, falling till one of the paramedics saw Leigh Roy coming towards them.

"Quick, we need a hand over here," called one paramedic.

Two fellas raced over to the stumbling Leigh Roy. Leigh Roy had made it and collapsed in a heap. He was dehydrated as well as severely concussed. The main road back to camp was clear, one of the only roads on site that hadn't been damaged. All employees in the workshop maintenance had now been accounted for and the supervisors notified.

Now the story goes back to Alfred and the emu saga. Alfred had jumped out of his fuel cart when realised it was an earthquake. As he jumped, he must have knocked his head. He was conscious and managed to walk, dazed, to the embankment. In his state, he began singing his blue skies song. One of the passing operator's twin cabs rushing to safety from the pit had seen Alfred and pulled him in, taking him to the side road of the maintenance crib hut. In passing, there was another fitter running. Looking behind, he tripped and fell over the embankment. Getting out of the vehicle, Alfred stumbled and fell backwards on his tailbone on a hard piece of coal. This was no emu. Yes, wildlife was running to higher or less dangerous ground. It was a figment of Alfred's imagination.

This would be Alfred's last assignment, as, like the rest of the miners' bobsled team, the royalties would kick in from the world promotion of this metal alloy.

It would be the last time for Leigh Roy as part of the team and its spoils to be on site.

They would evalute the damage after the tremors had subsided. The roads would be repaired and mining operations would carry on.

This was perfect timing now for Alfred to go home to his castle, to his lovely Margareta, his happy neighbours and of course the internal construction of the medieval shopping facilities and aquatic centre he had promised Ikav as a business partner. And the greenies. The so-called promised reservation where they would be happy and fenced off. There would be no need for them to be a public nuisance. They could live in their modified tree huts like Robinson Crusoe, have their own gardens, running water and of course no electricity, just open fires. They had cared so much for the environment to stop coal production that was used for producing steel and power generation, they didn't need electricity or car transportation, as these were commodities that helped produce transportation as well.

Matter of fact, you had to earn your way into this reservation. It came with a price. I'll let you think about that one.

Alfred and Leigh Roy did recover from their concussions. When Leigh Roy and Alfred were checked by the flying doctors and were certified fit, it was time to go home.

The D crew team and the rest of the world's fastest mining team with operators from over the other side were checked for traumas. This was a company policy after a major emergency.

Trevor Keen, Drew, Ernie, the quiet Roger and the gentle giant Ikav all had dreams of their own to conquer. They would remain a team or you could say a band of brothers. Yes, Alfred had been a good influence on them all and they valued that.

Nandi mining would go on to be one of the biggest coal mine producers in the area and the company would go on to make millions from Alfred's bobsled idea, which led to the production of a very strong and light alloy.

Leigh Roy had pledged to get his rocket engine go-cart racing when he got home. With a bit of thought and minimising his adrenaline rush, Leigh Roy was working on proving safety on his extreme racing techniques. He realised if he kept on pushing limits, not boundaries something not so good would happen to him. Leigh Roy did get to test his jet powered go-cart on Alfred's unregistered drag strip and, like Bert Munroe all those years on the salt flats of Bonneville, broke the world record, as mentioned previously, on his 1920s Indian modified motorcycle. Well, Leigh Roy did break a world go-cart record with a jet engine mounted to the back without killing himself.

Yes, there were many more challenges in Alfred's life to come, but as you can see from his story how he handles life's challenges, the world is a better place.

Alfred would go on to public speaking, giving advice to youth, become an accredited motivational speaker, and yes, open his castle grounds to the public with special venues of entertainment. The Rockhampton area would become an established tourist area in Queensland, thanks to Alfred Chuck Norris's dream of being a castle owner operator who had the initiative to take on power companies and build his own power generation systems, supplying the local community at a discounted rate.

Yes, one man had a dream when others laughed. Look now who is laughing all the way to the bank.

I wouldn't be surprised if Alfred opens his own bank in the future, backing his currency with gold.

Alfred would one day leave a legacy of his accomplishments and all the people that had and he had that would impact many lives. Yes, when the going gets tough, the tough get going.

Margareta enjoyed the thought of Alfred coming home for good, not having to worry about him when he went off to drive his fuel cart.

By the way, when they did find Alfred's fuel cart, it was squashed in the ground like a sardine can from the earthquake. The heavy vehicles left abandoned on the haul roads came out with minor damage.

Alfred lived on these principles:

When life gives you lemons, squirt someone in the eye.

Be happy, it drives people crazy.

The question isn't who is going to let me, it's who is going to stop me.

This is Alfred's Story, a Queenslander, a man who thinks

outside the square when he found what square was, a man of ambition and determination.

The man who knew too much...

Richard Stewart is a native of New Zealand. He has worked as an electrician, pilot, and miner. This is his fourth book.